Hero After Midnight

A Gibson Hollow Prequel

Kait Nolan

Author's Note

ATTENTION: I NEED YOU TO KNOW THIS IS A BACKSTORY PREQUEL THAT INHERENTLY ENDS ON A CLIFFHANGER.

Ahem, now that we've got that warning out of the way...

Welcome to Gibson Hollow. Well, the precursor to. This prequel doesn't take you there, but the rest of the series will.

This is a town where love is love, families come in all shapes, and everyone gets to show up exactly as they are—without fear, shame, or explanation.

In these pages, you won't find homophobia, racism, ableism, or cruelty rooted in fear of difference. Not because those things don't exist in the world—but because they don't belong in *this* one.

Here, drag queens are fairy godparents. Queer joy is sacred. Neurodivergence and chronic illness are woven into the rhythm of daily life. And no one's humanity is up for debate.

Gibson Hollow isn't a fantasy. It's a blueprint. It's the world I believe we *can* build—one book, one conversation, and one community at a time.

Thanks for stepping into it with me.

Love,

Kait

Chapter 1

Alia

"That's your reading for next week." Professor Kline rapped his knuckles on the table with the finality of a gavel strike. "And no, you can't skip it just because you think you understand privacy."

A couple of people laughed. I didn't.

I underlined the case name in my notes even though I'd already highlighted it twice. My fingers cramped around the pen, but it was easier to focus on that than the hollow gnaw of my stomach and the two-mile walk ahead of me.

Kline's voice cut through the rustling bags and the clatter of closing laptops. "Next week, we argue application, not history. Come prepared."

We always did. He ensured it by making an example of anyone who didn't, as though putting them on the stand in the courtroom he no longer presided over. After seeing it once in the second week of class, absolutely no one wanted to endure that humiliation.

Chairs scraped. Someone yawned loud enough to earn a glare from the retired judge turned professor. I closed my laptop and sat still for a beat, just long enough to breathe. Three classes, four hours at the firm, and a night seminar had turned my brain to mush. My feet ached in the boots that, while cute, had been a piss poor choice of footwear for the day. My to-do list still had eight unchecked boxes.

And instead of going home and falling face-first into bed, I was headed to a bar.

Because Jeff had asked.

I'd begged off to begin with because of my insane schedule and the coursework I'd still need to knock out when I got home. He hadn't made an issue of it, but he'd made The Face. That kicked puppy disappointed look I'd been seeing more and more over the past few months because this semester was kicking my ass. "No" was becoming my default answer instead of the exception, because I couldn't do anything to risk my academic scholarship.

I absolutely hated that face. Hated the creep of guilt it made me feel over doing what I needed to survive and keep all the many, many balls in the air. It was the guilt that had me turning toward the west side of campus that led into downtown instead of taking the shorter route back to the apartment I shared with my twin brother. I'd surprise Jeff, get a bite to eat, smooth ruffled feathers, then head home. I'd made an art form out of doing All The Things. I could do this, too.

After sitting through three hours of Constitutional Law and Civil Liberties, the walk gave me a chance to clear my head and stretch my legs. The October night air was cool and refreshing. Back home in Gibson Hollow, the nights would already be bordering on cold. Amazing what a few thousand feet of elevation could do. I missed the mountains, but I didn't mind Wellington. It was bigger than home but not quite a city. It had been a good place to spend the last two and a half years at Carolina Southern University. Close enough for visits, and far enough away that I got a break from the responsibilities of being the eldest of eight.

A handful of cars passed me as I crossed the bridge that separated CSU's campus from Wellington proper. Streetlights trailed along Main Street, illuminating the shopfronts of businesses long closed for the day. At the corner, I took a left and cut over two blocks to Ashby Street. The length of it was packed with vehicles and foot traffic, a stark contrast to the rest of Wellington. This was the student district, full of coffeeshops, bars, and other student hangouts that stayed open well after everything else shuttered.

Even from the corner, I could hear music and voices spilling from Whiskey Jack's. My whole body tensed. It was half-off loaded fries night, plus cheap drinks—guaranteed chaos. The scarred dance floor would be packed. Not my scene, but Jeff fed on that kind of energy. Everyone insisted him dragging me out was good for me. And usually, despite my raging introvert status, I ended up having a good time.

Bracing myself, I dragged open the door to the bar and stepped into a wall of sound. It was like being hit by a tidal wave of input. Whimpering, I almost turned back around. He didn't actually expect me to come. I'd already said no. If I dipped now, he'd never know.

My stomach chose that moment to growl, reminding me that it had been more than nine hours since I'd had food. The loaded fries did sound good.

Just find Jeff and get a bite to eat. Then you can go home.

I began weaving my way through the crowd, scanning for my boyfriend. Whiskey Jack's drew the football crowd, so I saw quite a few familiar faces. My brother, Bodie, played guard for CSU on a football scholarship. Jeff was one of his teammates —a linebacker for the Ravens. But he didn't seem to be hanging with any of the usual crowd tonight. I nodded greetings but ask anyone if they'd seen him. The last thing I wanted was to get pulled into conversation.

After a full circuit of the bar, I was about to give up when I spotted his jersey at the edge of the dance floor. Barrett. Number 43. God bless his desire for attention. I took half a step in his direction before I registered the rest of what I was seeing in the flashing lights of the bar. He was caught in a lip lock with some other girl. And it definitely wasn't a case of some random drunk girl throwing herself at him. He wasn't trying to push her off. His arms were wrapped around her, one hand buried in her hair. No effort to hide. In fact, he seemed very intent on examining her tonsils with his tongue. Just out there for everyone to see. As if I didn't exist. As if we hadn't been dating for the better part of a year.

I froze.

For a long moment, my brain refused to catch up with my eyes, like if I just stood still long enough, the scene in front of me would rewrite itself. But Jeff was still there, arms locked around someone who definitely wasn't me, kissing her like he was starving.

The world didn't go silent—if anything, it got

louder. The pounding music, the laughter, the screech of a stool scraping the floor behind me—it all surged in a dizzy, disorienting rush. I wasn't invisible. People had seen me come in. People saw this. And if I did anything—if I so much as flinched —there'd be whispers and speculation and looks.

A wild part of me wanted to march across the room and yank him away, demand to know how long this had been going on, and ask if he was really so stupid that he thought no one would tell me. I imagined the scene, every eye swiveling to watch. His friends, my brother's teammates, the girls who already hated me. Everyone would be watching the show.

I couldn't do it.

Not because I wasn't angry—I was. Not because I didn't deserve an answer—I did. But because giving him that moment, that attention, would make it worse. It would make me the story, not him. I could already feel the heat of too many eyes, the whisper of gossip winding itself into place.

No. I wouldn't give him the satisfaction.

So I turned on my heel, head down, heart clawing its way up my throat—

—and crashed directly into a wall.

Only it wasn't a wall.

It was a man.

Big. Solid.

Two hands came up fast to catch my arms, grounding me with a gentle, instinctive grip. "Hey— easy."

I looked up.

Ramsey.

Of course. Of course, it was him.

His brows drew together the instant he saw my face—just a flicker of concern before his gaze shifted over my shoulder. I didn't have to turn to know what he was seeing.

His jaw tightened and rage leapt into his eyes, even as his fingers flexed around my arms, as if his grip could somehow protect me from what was happening. "Alia..."

Hearing my name in that quiet tone cracked something in my chest. Not enough to break. Just enough to ache.

I shook my head and stepped back. I couldn't talk. Not here. Not yet. And especially not to the one person I really didn't want to see me like this.

A muscle jumped in that scruff-covered jaw, and his hands curled to fists as he glanced back toward the spectacle on the dance floor. I had five brothers. I knew exactly what a man who wanted to beat the shit out of someone looked like. A part of me wanted to let him. But that would bring even more attention to this, and I couldn't bear it.

My hand shot out, curling around Ramsey's

muscled forearm. "Please, don't. It's not worth the scene. I just want to go home."

His fingers flexed and curled several times before he seemed to get a grip on his temper. With a short nod, he pressed a hand to the small of my back. "C'mon. I'll walk you."

Outside, the cold hit harder than it had on the walk over. The wind wasn't strong, just enough to knife through my thin sweater and sting my cheeks. I wrapped my arms around myself, fingers tucked into the opposite sleeves. My backpack shifted with the motion, biting into my shoulders with familiar weight.

Funny how I hadn't been cold before. Not even walking from class. But now it felt as if the heat had bled out of me entirely. I was frozen and humiliated, and somehow the shame made it worse. Like I deserved the cold for being stupid enough to walk into that bar in the first place.

I should've trusted my instincts. Should've stayed home. Should've seen it coming.

I hated this.

I hated *him*.

And most of all, I hated how badly I still wanted to cry. Worse, how badly I wanted to throw myself into Ramsey's arms and bury my face against the massive wall of his shoulder to do it. He was Bodie's best friend. Basically another brother to me.

That was how he'd always treated me. It was too damned bad my heart had never gotten the memo. I'd had a hideous crush on him almost from the moment we'd met freshman year. Not that he knew. And I'd bite my tongue off before admitting it.

We didn't talk as we walked. The music from Whiskey Jack's faded behind us, replaced by the steady scuff of our steps on the sidewalk and the occasional rumble of a passing car. Ramsey didn't push. He didn't ask questions or try to force conversation. He just kept pace with me, a solid wall at my side.

That silent, steady presence only made me feel worse. Because of course he could tell I wasn't okay. I wasn't that good an actress. How much of an idiot did he think I was? Had he known about this?

I thought about that flash of rage back at the bar. No, he definitely hadn't known. If he had, he'd have told Bodie, and between the two of them, probably nobody would've found the body.

About halfway down the block, Ramsey paused. I glanced up just as he tugged his hoodie over his head and held it out to me.

"Here."

I stared at it for a second, doing my level best not to focus on how it left him in nothing but a gray T-shirt that clung to his muscled frame like it had been painted on. The hoodie was warm from his body, soft from a thousand washes, and I hesitated because slipping it on felt like something... more.

But my teeth were starting to chatter, and I wasn't about to let that be the thing that finally broke me.

So I took it with shaking hands, slipping my backpack off so I could pull the sweatshirt over my head. It was massive on me—of course it was—and it smelled like him. Like soap and cedar and something I couldn't name but instinctively knew was Ramsey.

I shoved my hands into the too-long sleeves and crossed my arms tighter, sinking into the cocoon of fabric. It wasn't a hug. Not really. But it was close enough to pretend.

He didn't say anything else. Just picked up my bag and slung it over one shoulder before resuming his position beside me, leaving exactly enough space for me to breathe but never drifting far as we continued to walk.

And I...

I spiraled.

The silence let the thoughts loose, tumbling fast and cruel. I should've seen it. I'd known something was off for weeks. The distracted texts, the way Jeff's smiles didn't quite reach his eyes. I'd told myself it was school. Football. Stress. That I was the problem, saying no too often, being too tired, too busy, too serious.

God, had I done this? Had I just worn him down?

I felt sick and small and so, so stupid.

I didn't want Ramsey to see me like this—curled in on myself, locked in my own head, blaming myself for someone else's betrayal. But I didn't know how to *not* feel it. It was like all my years of holding it together weren't enough to hold back the flood this time.

We turned the corner toward my apartment, the familiar stoop just a block away. The lights were still off upstairs. Bodie was probably still at the gym or out with teammates.

Thank God.

Because he'd want to know all the details, and aside from the fact that I didn't have it in me to stop him from haring off to do something foolish, like beating the shit out of Jeff, I couldn't take one more person looking at me like I might fall apart. Not when I was barely keeping the cracks from showing.

We climbed the steps in silence. I pulled the key from my front pocket, fingers fumbling with the lock more than they should've. Ramsey waited behind me, quiet and steady as ever.

The deadbolt clicked. I pushed the door open

and stepped just inside the threshold, then paused, hand still on the knob. My voice came out soft, barely audible over the rustle of trees in the breeze. "Thanks for walking me home."

I didn't look at him when I said it. I couldn't. My eyes were locked somewhere around his chest, unable to lift higher because if I did—if I saw pity or concern or anything too gentle—I might actually shatter.

I was supposed to be the one who had it together. The one who didn't fall apart.

But he didn't flinch. Didn't fumble for meaningless platitude. He just stepped forward, setting my backpack just inside the door before curling his big hand gently around my shoulder. The kindness of the gesture almost had me collapsing against him.

"Get some sleep. It's gonna be okay."

The low rumble of his voice didn't sound like false hope. Just a quiet certainty. As if he knew I wouldn't let this take me down.

I nodded, but still didn't look at him. "Night."

Then I shut the door before I could do something stupid like let loose the flood of tears burning behind my eyes.

I toed off my boots and tucked my bag out of the path of the entryway. The living room was dark and still, untouched since this morning. I didn't bother with lights. Just went upstairs to my bedroom, shut the door behind me, and collapsed face-first onto my bed.

The scream that tore out of me was muffled by the comforter, but it was all heat and shame and humiliation. Not heartbreak. I wasn't grieving Jeff. I wasn't even sure I liked him all that much anymore. I hadn't been building a life or a future with him. He'd been a placeholder. Someone to go out with. To have fun with before I got down to the serious business of the rest of my life.

But God, I was furious. Mortified. And so god-damned tired.

I rolled onto my side and curled up, arms crossed over my chest. That's when I realized I was still wearing Ramsey's hoodie. I'd forgotten to give it back.

Of course I had.

The fabric bunched around me like borrowed armor. I pulled the sleeves tighter, tucked my hands into the pockets, and buried my face in the collar.

It smelled like him. The warmth of it seeped into cracks I hadn't let anyone see. Not even him.

Especially not him.

I pressed my face deeper into the hoodie and let myself breathe, just once, like I hadn't been able to all night.

Then I closed my eyes and fell asleep, wrapped in borrowed fabric and a truth I didn't want to name.

Chapter 2

Ramsey

I sat in my truck, parked at the curb down the street from Bodie and Alia's apartment. The engine was off, windows cracked just enough to let in the bite of October. I hadn't slept. Not even a little. My body was dead tired, but my brain refused to quit. It kept looping back to last night like it was trying to burn every second into my skull.

I'd come so damned close to going back.

After I'd walked Alia home, after I'd made sure her light was on and that she was safe behind a locked door, I'd stood in this exact spot with my hands clenched and the overwhelming urge to march back into Whiskey Jack's and do what she hadn't let me do in the moment.

Wreck Jeff Barrett.

It would've been easy. One swing. One hit. I had the reach to put him on the ground before he even saw it coming. Not that a single punch would be remotely sufficient retribution. The guy deserved to be beaten bloody for what he'd done to her. But then I'd heard her voice again—that quiet, frayed "Please, don't. I just want to go home." Like it hurt her to say it. Like keeping me from throwing a punch was the last bit of control she had.

So I didn't.

I didn't, and it killed me.

Because every time I closed my eyes, I saw her face when she ran into me—shocked, pale, like someone had pulled the floor out from under her. She hadn't said anything, hadn't even flinched, but it had been there in her eyes. Hurt she hadn't meant anyone to see.

And yeah, I'd felt it. That sharp, hot twist in my gut. Not just because of what that asshole had done, but because she'd looked like she was trying to hold the whole damn world together with duct tape and willpower, and she wasn't going to let him—or anyone else—see her break.

She hadn't cried. She hadn't yelled. She'd just walked out, spine straight and eyes dry, and that probably gutted me more than if she'd thrown a drink in his face. That was Alia. Strong as hell. Always handling it, even when she shouldn't have to.

I'd never liked Barrett—the smug, arrogant prick, with his fake charm and desperate need for attention. But I figured if Alia saw something in him, maybe he had some redeeming qualities I was missing. Hell, she'd been with him for almost a year. I'd wanted to believe she was happy. That he was good to her. That she'd picked someone who deserved her.

Clearly I'd been wrong.

Now all I could think about was what she must've felt walking into that bar and seeing him publicly, unapologetically disrespecting her. As if she didn't matter. As if she didn't even exist.

He hadn't known she was there. That much had been painfully obvious. But plenty of others had seen. I wondered if someone had told him after she left. I wondered if she'd called or texted to end things after she'd gone inside last night. There was no question it was over. She'd never take the asshat back after that. I just wasn't sure if she'd gotten to it yet.

I shifted in my seat and rubbed a hand over my face. The sun was barely up. Her apartment was still dark, except for the soft porch light over the stoop. I wasn't here to talk to her. That wasn't the plan. I'd made myself stay put because I didn't want to make her feel worse. She'd been mortified last night. The last thing she needed was to see me hovering, reminding her of everything she was trying not to feel.

Still... I couldn't leave without seeing her. Just once. Just to make sure she was okay. So I sat there in the truck, engine off, watching the front door like it might offer some kind of answer. And when it finally opened, and she stepped outside, I felt my grip tighten on the wheel.

She looked tired. Not just sleep-deprived, but worn thin—as if she hadn't quite patched herself back together from last night. But she was up. Hair tied back in that no-nonsense way of hers. Backpack slung over one shoulder.

And she was wearing my hoodie.

It hit me like a linebacker.

The thing absolutely swallowed her—sleeves past her fingertips, hem brushing her thighs—but she wore it like it was armor. Like maybe it gave her just enough protection or comfort to keep going. It was mine, but it looked like hers now. Like maybe she needed it. Like maybe, somehow, I'd given her something that helped.

That thought lodged itself somewhere beneath my ribs and wouldn't let go.

I didn't get out. Didn't call to her. She didn't need a witness to how hard she was fighting to be okay. She needed space. Quiet. Normalcy. So I let her have it. Kept my hands easy on the wheel and just watched her walk away.

And maybe I shouldn't have cared so much that she kept the hoodie.

But I did.

She turned the corner and disappeared from view, but the weight of the moment lingered. I let it hang for a beat—then pulled myself back to the task at hand. I hadn't driven out here just to watch her walk to class. As much as I wanted to stay lost in thoughts I had no business entertaining, there was a reason I'd come this early. One that couldn't wait.

Once she was out of sight, I got out of the truck, letting the door shut softly behind me. My boots crunched the gravel as I jogged to the apartment. I rapped my knuckles against the door. A beat passed. Then another. It was early yet, and Bodie didn't have class for two more hours. He didn't share his sister's early-bird habits. I knocked again, harder this time, and finally heard slow, reluctant movement inside.

The door cracked open to reveal Bodie, looking like someone had dragged him out of bed and through a wind tunnel. A pair of cutoff CSU sweatpants hung low on his hips. His T-shirt was inside out, and his brown hair—usually trimmed close—was sticking up in all directions like he'd gone toe-to-toe with a pillow and lost.

He blinked at me, squinting against the morning light that made it past my shoulders to stab him straight in the eyes. "Jesus, man. It's not even eight."

I didn't smile or offer up a joke. "You're lucky I like you."

That earned a grunt, but the corners of his mouth twitched like he wanted to smirk. It died fast when he saw my face. "You good?"

I was so far from good, I couldn't even begin to describe it. "Let me inside."

He instantly stepped back. "What's going on, man? Something happen to your mom?"

I shook my head. "No. No, she's fine. You seen your sister yet this morning?" I knew the answer was probably no, as I'd clearly dragged him from bed.

The question snapped him the rest of the way awake. "No. Heard her leave a little while ago." His posture sharpened, sleep draining off him like water. "Why?"

I didn't ease into it. "She caught Barrett cheating last night at Whiskey Jack's."

For just a second, Bodie went still. Then he exploded. "He did what?"

His voice cracked like a whip, and he'd already halfway turned toward the hallway, muscles bunched, fists clenched. I could practically see the smoke rising off him. "Tell me he's not still breathing."

He disappeared briefly into his room. Drawers slammed. He came back out a second later with socks in one hand and a shoe flying across the floor from the other.

I stepped in his path and caught his shoulder. "Hey."

He yanked away like I'd burned him. "Don't you dare try to talk me down right now, man. He cheated on my sister. You know what she's been dealing with this semester. You know how much she put into that relationship. She doesn't ask for shit from anybody and—"

"I *know*." I kept my voice calm but firm, matching his volume without raising my own. "You think I didn't want to break him in half? You think I didn't almost do it last night?"

That made him pause. "Wait, you were there?"

"Yeah. I ran into her. Or she ran into me, I guess." I shoved a hand through my hair. "She saw him, Bodie. On the dance floor. Making out with some girl like she was the one he'd been dating all this time. Didn't even try to hide it."

"What did Alia do?"

"Nothing. You know how she is. She wouldn't have wanted the scene. She hates being the center of any kind of attention, and if she'd confronted him there, it would have been all over campus by this morning. So she just turned around and walked away. No scene. No tears. Just left."

"Why didn't you do something?"

I knew he didn't mean it like an accusation. Not really. We were both protectors where Alia was concerned. It was our shared job, even if only one of us knew how far that ran. "I'd have happily pounded him into the floor, but she asked me not to make a scene. Said she just wanted to go home. So I walked her to make sure she got here okay."

Bodie stared at me, jaw tight, the fury barely leashed behind his eyes. "She tell you anything after?"

"No. And I didn't ask. She looked wrecked, man. I figured you should hear it from me before you do something that puts you on academic probation."

His nostrils flared. His hands clenched and un-clenched at his sides. "What do you want me to do, Ramsey? Pretend like I'm not ready to throw that motherfucker through a wall?"

"No," I said quietly. "But we *have* to consider what *she* wants."

His brows drew together. "You don't seriously think she'll stay with this asshole after this?"

"No. And I don't actually think she'd object to him being taught a lesson. But it needs to be done in such a way that it doesn't blow back on her. She'll want to fly under the radar on all of this, give people as little to talk about as possible. You go storming into the locker room, it becomes a team problem. A university problem. He's not worth that."

Bodie paced a tight circle around the living room, breath heaving like a bull ready to charge, and I knew it cost him not to act right now. He swung back to face me. "You can't expect me to do nothing."

"I don't. Look, the bastard humiliated her. I wanted to break his jaw for it. Still do. But she didn't want that, and I wasn't about to do something she didn't ask for." I let out a breath, trying to keep my voice even. "But that doesn't mean we let it slide."

He stopped pacing. "What are you saying?"

"That there's a right way to handle this, and we need to settle the details before we see him at practice this afternoon."

We exchanged a long look, one of those silent communications that made us an unstoppable offensive line on the field. Understanding dawned on his face.

On a long breath, his shoulders relaxed, the decision made. "Okay, then." He paused. "You want coffee?"

I thought of the thermos in the truck that I'd

been sipping on for the past two hours. It was gonna take more than that to keep me going through the rest of my day. "Wouldn't say no."

As Bodie puttered around the little galley kitchen, adding water and grounds to the coffeemaker, I settled back against the table.

Alia deserved better than the likes of Jeff Barrett. She deserved the fucking world, and I should've said something years ago. But given her brother was my best friend, that made my less than brotherly feelings for her more than a little sticky. He had no idea. Neither did she. And that was how it probably had to stay.

I couldn't tell her what she meant to me. Couldn't hold her like I wanted to. Couldn't do a damn thing to fix the hurt in her eyes.

But this? Keeping her brother from going off half-cocked? Finding a way to put the hurt on Jeff without making a bigger mess for Alia? This I could do for her.

Chapter 3

Alia

The sun was too bright, the bleachers too cold, and the heat from my coffee had long since seeped through the cardboard cup. My laptop sat open on my thighs, screen dimmed but untouched. I'd told myself I'd get through my Con Law reading while Bodie was at practice, but so far all I'd managed to do was reread the same sentence twelve times without absorbing a single word because my brain was still circling around Jeff's reply to my breakup text, fanning the flames of the temper I basically never let off leash.

That would've been easier if my eyes didn't keep drifting to the field, where the man who'd cheated on me was running drills like nothing had happened.

I absolutely didn't want to be here. If I'd had my own car, I wouldn't have been. But I shared one with Bodie, and he had football practice—as he did most afternoons. I hadn't had a chance to tell him everything that had happened yet. I could have texted him and asked him to get a ride home with Ramsey, but then he'd have wanted to know why, and I didn't want to get into all of that over text. I also didn't want to face Ramsey again after last night. So here I was, perched in the stands like I was fine.

"Okay." Blair slid her sunglasses down her nose so she could peer at me over the top of them. "You gonna tell me why you're trying to burn holes in your screen with your mind?"

I blew out a slow breath and finally looked at my bestie. Chill, stylish, and sparkly, she was everything I wasn't. We'd met first week of freshman year and immediately hit it off. We'd been inseparable ever since. She lounged beside me like this was her own private spa, one long leg tucked under the other, bright pink nails wrapped around a drink from the campus cafe. She was the only person I could stand to be around right now.

"I saw Jeff last night."

Blair raised a brow at my flat tone. "Like, on purpose or...?"

"At Whiskey Jack's." I glanced away, fingers

tightening around my cup. "With his tongue down someone else's throat."

Her gasp was cinematic. "No. No! That walking shit stain! Are you kidding me?"

"I wish." I stared out over the field, at the lines painted across the grass, the players gathered at midfield. "He wasn't even trying to hide it."

By the time I finished telling her the rest of it, she practically vibrated with righteous fury. "You should've dumped a drink on him."

"That would've meant making a scene. I'd rather set him on fire quietly."

Blair's eyes flashed. "We could key his truck. Or his soul. Your choice."

Despite myself, I huffed a short laugh. I had to appreciate her well-developed sense of vengeance.

She sobered. "Seriously though. You just left?"

"I just left. Ramsey walked me home."

"Ramsey was there?"

"I literally walked into him when I turned to leave." And it had been like hitting a massive, warm, really good smelling wall. Not that I was thinking about that. "He saw, too."

And God, that made my cheeks burn with further embarrassment. Certainly, plenty of other people there had seen. But there'd been no one else whose opinion I actually cared about. How foolish did I look for being with Jeff in the first place?

"And he didn't do anything either?"

"Oh, he would have. But that would have been more of a scene, and the last thing his football career needs is an arrest for assault."

God, that would kill his mom. And who knew what kind of legal fees would be involved in something like that? I wasn't saddling him with that. Not even for the satisfaction of seeing my ex flattened.

Blair scowled. "I wish I'd been there. I'd have clawed his face off."

"Seriously, B, he's not worth ruining your manicure." But the mental image of my statuesque bestie opening a very stylish can of whoop-ass did give me the warm fuzzies. What did that say about me?

She draped an arm around my shoulders. "You're worth it, my darling. Have you at least solidly ended things?"

I leaned into the embrace. "I texted him this morning. Told him we were done."

"And?"

I pulled out my phone, brought up the message thread, and handed it over.

Blair read the message exchange—his smug little reply about how it was 'no skin off his nose' and how we'd 'barely been together anyway'—and looked like she was ready to commit an actual felony.

She shoved my phone back into my hand. "I

swear to God. What an absolute hemorrhoid of a human."

"It didn't wreck me," I said quietly, more to myself than to her. "It pissed me off."

"Good. Pissed off is way better than heartbroken."

"I wasn't in love with him. I wasn't even close. Truthfully, a part of me is relieved. I have so much to juggle this year with my course load, keeping my scholarship, doing my internship at the firm. I honestly don't have time to date. Now I don't have to feel like he's another thing to add to my checklist."

Blair gave me a long look out of perfectly winged eyes. "Baby, if that's how you were thinking about your relationship, y'all definitely weren't doing it right."

I snorted. "It's further proof we weren't actually a good fit. I think I knew that. I just... didn't feel like dealing with the drama of ending it or with getting back out there to date anyone else. The more fool me."

"You're not a fool. Not even a little bit. But maybe you aren't exactly in the right headspace for dating."

"At this point, I feel like avoiding the whole thing until after law school. I'm too busy."

"Let's put a pin in that before you make a

sweeping declaration that's going to last the next four and a half years."

The corner of my lips curved faintly as I let Blair's words settle around me like a comforting blanket.

My eyes drifted out to the field, where the team was lined up for a scrimmage. Bodie was holding down the line at left guard, Ramsey split off the end in position as tight end—Thunder and Lightning, as the team called them. It started as a joke, something the announcers and campus sports accounts latched onto. But it stuck because it was true. When they moved together, it wasn't just offense—it was controlled demolition.

I'd always loved watching Ramsey play. Quietly. Secretly. The way some people appreciated fine art or ballet or flawless mechanics. There was something mesmerizing about seeing him move. Calculated. Focused. Ruthlessly efficient. Like a predator who knew exactly when and where to strike. It shouldn't have been attractive—brutality dressed up as athleticism—but something about it always hit me square in the chest. Blair would've called it competence porn. I called it beautiful to watch.

Not that I'd ever say that out loud.

The ball snapped.

Jeff, lined up as outside linebacker, came in hot on a blitz off the edge.

He didn't get far.

In the space of a breath, Bodie peeled off his block like it was choreographed, and Ramsey was already there to meet him, the two of them converging with ruthless precision. The hit landed like a thunderclap—shoulder to ribs, legs taken out clean—and Jeff crumpled like a folding chair.

I flinched, my whole body recoiling, coffee sloshing dangerously close to the rim of my cup. Football was a rough game—God knew I'd grown up watching enough of it—but that had been more than a clean tackle.

That had been personal.

Jeff didn't move right away. For a second, I actually thought he might stay down. But eventually, he rolled to his knees, helmet askew, blinking like he couldn't quite remember where he was.

"Yikes," Blair muttered beside me. "Someone's making enemies on the field."

I didn't answer. My eyes were locked on the two players walking calmly back to the line. Bodie and Ramsey, side by side, the very picture of "nothing to see here."

Only I knew these men, and there absolutely was something to see.

Another snap. Another blitz.

Jeff tried to cut inside this time.

Bodie met him low, Ramsey came in high. Their timing was flawless. The impact was bone-deep—loud enough to echo—and Jeff hit the turf again like the ground had reached up and yanked him down.

This time, he stayed there longer.

When he finally shoved himself up, he was clearly limping, one hand clutching his side. He yanked off his helmet and hurled words at one of the coaches—too far away for me to make out, but the tone said enough. A warning shout came from the sideline, but no one got pulled. No flags. No whistles.

Everything looked clean enough.

And yet, somehow, Jeff was the only one who looked wrecked.

If you didn't know any better.

But I did.

This wasn't merely practice. This wasn't bad luck or even an unlucky matchup.

This was calculated. Planned.

My stomach fluttered—not with nerves, but something wilder, sharper, more visceral.

Ramsey had told Bodie. He had to have. And this—this was retaliation. Silent and vicious. Carried out in plain sight. It was exactly the kind of justice I would've dreamed up if I had the physical ability to lay someone out on the fifty-yard line.

Perfectly legal. Painfully satisfying. And absolutely impossible to trace back to me.

Beside me, Blair leaned forward, her posture shifting from relaxed to laser-focused, eyes narrowed behind her oversized sunglasses. "You're seeing this too, right? That's not normal practice brutality."

"Nope."

"Ramsey told him."

I didn't even hesitate. "Yep."

We sat in silence for a beat, watching Jeff limp back to the huddle with all the grace of a sore loser.

And for the first time since last night, I didn't feel small. Or humiliated. Or like the punchline to some mean-spirited joke.

I felt seen.

Not pitied. Not rescued. But avenged in a way that kept my dignity intact.

It was beyond satisfying. It felt like justice.

And God help me, I wasn't even a little sorry.

As the players reset on the field, my gaze drifted instinctively to the far end of the offensive line— drawn there like a compass needle. Ramsey stood tall and unshaken as he waited for the next snap. Calm. Controlled. Like nothing phased him.

But I remembered last night.

His hand had been warm and steady at the small of my back, guiding me home without a word of pressure or questions. Only quiet presence. It had been the softest touch, but it grounded me more than I could explain. I hadn't even realized how much I'd needed that—how brittle I'd felt— until his fingers brushed against my spine like he was holding me together without making it obvious.

And the hoodie.

I glanced down, momentarily remembering the weight of it last night as I'd pulled it over my head. Too big. Soft. Still carrying the warmth of him and that clean, woodsy scent. It had felt like a barrier against the world. A hug I didn't have to ask for.

Comfort I hadn't known how to receive.

And before I'd shut the door behind me, he'd said, "It's gonna be okay."

Not with forced cheer or vague platitudes. Simply a quiet certainty that had somehow carved space in my chest where the panic had been sitting.

I swallowed hard.

What would've happened if I'd stayed on that porch one second longer?

Would he have followed me inside? Said something else? Reached for me the way I'd wanted to reach for him?

The thought barely formed before I shut it down, stuffed it back into the place I kept all the complicated feelings I didn't have time to unpack. That wasn't what last night had been about. He was Bodie's best friend. He was being kind. That was all.

Still, the weight of his voice lingered in my mind.

It's gonna be okay.

What was it about him saying it that made me think... maybe it would be?

The whistle blew again, and bodies shifted across the field, but I wasn't watching anymore.

I pulled my laptop closer and opened a blank document—not the brief I needed to draft for my internship or the notes I needed to finish for Con Law. A fresh, empty screen.

My fingers hovered over the keys. Then I began to type.

He didn't see it at first. The cocky, careless boy, too busy stumbling through the dark, grinning like he owned the night. But the trees knew. The wind knew. And something else—something old and clawed and hungry—knew too. It stalked on silent paws, all sinew and shadow, and watched him trip over his own arrogance. When it struck, it didn't roar. It didn't snarl. It just sank its teeth in deep, relishing the warm copper tang of blood filling its mouth and the high, thin scream of terror that split the night before it dragged him into the earth.

I paused, rereading the paragraph. It was ridiculous and savage and maybe a little bit dramatic—but God, it felt good.

"Girl." Blair leaned over, peering at my screen behind the blonde curtain of her hair. "That's some Greek-tragedy level vengeance. I approve. You should keep going."

"I think I will." I tapped the space bar once. "I think it would be cathartic."

The wind picked up, tugging loose strands of my hair into my face. Down on the field, another whistle blew. Another snap.

Another hit. Jeff hit the turf with a grunt that echoed across the stands.

This time, I didn't flinch. I kept typing, smiling at the sound of the keys clicking steadily beneath my fingers.

Chapter 4

Alia

The apartment was quiet, save for the low hum of the TV from the living room where Bodie and Ramsey were watching some sitcom rerun. The noise of the laugh tracks barely registered as I sat on the edge of my bed, staring at the dress hanging from a hook on the closet door. The purple shimmer caught the soft light filtering in from the window, the fabric looking every bit as powerful and elegant as the day I'd tried it on. It was the kind of dress that demanded attention without trying. Bold lines. Clean structure. And absolutely unlike anything I'd ever tried to wear.

I had no idea why I'd bought it, really. But it had felt important, so I'd worked for it. Extra shifts at the firm. Weekends I couldn't afford to lose, doing coffee runs and redlines just to squirrel away enough for something that would make me feel... different. Something I'd picked for me. Not to impress anyone else. Not even Jeff.

But now, looking at it made my stomach knot.

The mask sat on my desk beside it, resting in the open velvet box Uncle Dee had mailed it in with three layers of tissue paper and a note that said, "You're gonna turn heads, baby girl. Go give 'em whiplash." Metallic purple and black feathers arched like wings around the edges, the detailing delicate but dramatic—almost regal. It was beautiful. Powerful. Made with love.

And now it was just another thing Jeff had ruined.

I swallowed hard and looked away. He hadn't even taken the moment from me directly. He'd tainted it by association, made it feel pointless. Like I'd been dressing up for a fantasy that no longer existed. I didn't want to walk into that masquerade party, pretending like I wasn't nursing the bruises to my pride.

I could go out to the living room and try to lose myself in whatever the boys were watching. But I wasn't feeling amused, and I wasn't ready to actually face Ramsey. I hadn't seen him in more than passing since the night he'd walked me home. Hadn't given him back his hoodie. I was working on admitting to myself that I didn't intend to unless he asked for it directly. What did it say that I was keeping my brother's best friend's sweatshirt as a piece of emotional support clothing?

Nothing I wanted to talk to my brother about, so that same hoodie was hidden in the corner of my closet, where Bodie wouldn't see. And if he somehow found it, I'd claim it was one of his that I'd stolen.

The front door slammed open with all the subtlety of a Broadway entrance.

"I'm just saying," Blair's voice rang down the hall, loud and unapologetic, "your door was unlocked, which felt like an invitation to save your life."

Startled, I blinked and sat up straighter.

"Hey, boys!" she called toward the living room. "Try not to miss me too much while I go rescue your favorite girl from the brink."

A muffled reply from Bodie, something sarcastic but good-natured, followed. I didn't catch Ramsey's voice, but that didn't mean I wasn't straining for it.

The sounds of rustling bags and ice clinking in plastic cups followed. There was no mistaking the trademark chaos energy of Blair in full dramatic flight.

"I also come bearing caffeine." Her voice carried as she dropped something onto the kitchen counter with a theatrical thunk.

I scrubbed a hand over my eyes and rose slowly, padding barefoot down the hall. As I stepped into the kitchen, my gaze flicked toward the living room beyond. I caught the barest glimpse of Ramsey reclined on the couch, profile sharp in the blue glow of the television. Only a flicker of him before I made myself look away.

Blair stood at the counter like some caffeine-fueled avenging angel, her enormous sunglasses still on despite being indoors, one hand on her hip, the other holding out a cup like she was bestowing a blessing.

She eyed me up and down. "I brought a bag of emotionally supportive bullshit you're absolutely going to let me use on your face."

Despite myself, a breath of laughter escaped me, a single exhale that felt lighter than anything I'd let out all day. Blair had a gift for cutting through the fog. For showing up at exactly the right moment and being too loud, too much, and somehow exactly what I needed.

"I wasn't expecting company."

"Clearly." She pressed the cup into my hands. "And clearly, you needed it."

She turned back to her canvas tote, pulling out something wrapped in silk and something else that crinkled like a makeup pouch full of secrets. I didn't ask what any of it was. I simply stood there, holding iced coffee, watching her commandeer my kitchen like she lived here.

And in that moment—with my heart still scraped raw and my mind a mess—I was so overwhelmed with love for her I almost couldn't speak. She didn't knock. Didn't ask. She showed up. Like she'd known I needed her before I did.

"Blair." My voice was low and wobbly.

She paused, looked up, and for a moment dropped the performance. "I got you. Now, let's go resurrect your sparkle."

Blair ushered me down the hall to my room. Her sunglasses were finally off, shoved into her thick mass of blonde hair. Her gaze swept the space, taking in the dress still hanging on the closet door and the open velvet box on my desk. Her eyes landed on the mask. She stepped toward it, reverent, as if she'd found some ancient artifact. She picked it up, turning it gently in her hands, brushing her thumb over the delicate filigree and plum-feather accents. "Your Uncle Dee absolutely outdid himself. That man has such a gift with costuming and design. I really must get him to teach me all his secrets."

The way she said it made my throat ache. Like

the thing still mattered. Like the magic was still there, waiting for me to claim it.

"It doesn't matter." I collapsed back onto the edge of my bed. "I'm not going."

She turned to face me with a single brow raised and a glint in her eye that should've been a warning. "Like hell you're not."

I pulled my knees up and wrapped my arms around them, gaze falling to the stretch of carpet between us. "I don't have the energy for that right now."

"Then borrow mine."

I huffed out something halfway between a scoff and a sigh.

Blair toed off her boots and shed her jacket, tossing it over the back of my desk chair like she was clocking in. She didn't wait for an invitation—just climbed up onto my bed and sat cross-legged beside me, fixing me with the kind of look that didn't leave room for bullshit.

She let the silence hang for a moment before she cut through it with surgical precision. "So, what's the real reason?"

I knew she wouldn't let it go. Not with the mask still in her lap and her eyes sharper than they had any right to be for someone who wore glitter eyeliner before noon.

I shifted, my hands curling around my sweating cup. "I don't have a date."

Blair scoffed. "That's the worst excuse I've ever heard you try to sell me. Try again."

"I'm serious."

"No, you're avoiding." She arched one brow and gave me the Look—the one that said she'd wait all day and drag every truth out of me like a dentist with a stubborn molar. "You're going to tell me the truth, sweet cheeks, or I'm going to start reading your Google search history aloud, and I know for a fact you looked up 'how to sue the universe' last week."

A reluctant laugh slipped out of me. It tasted like defeat and relief. "Fine." I leaned back against the headboard. "It's not about Jeff. Not really."

Blair stayed quiet, shifting to mirror me, her knees up, attention laser focused.

"I was so excited about that dress. For the masquerade." My voice went soft. "Not because of him. It wasn't about being one half of a cute couple or anything. I just... wanted to feel like someone."

Blair tilted her head. "You are someone."

"I know. But this—" I nodded toward the dress, still gleaming like temptation on my closet door. "This was supposed to be the first time I let myself really... take up space."

Her gaze softened. "Yeah, you don't do that. And girl, you *should.*"

That wasn't something I was comfortable with. I'd spent my whole life tucked into the margins—Bodie's quiet sister, the serious one, the responsible one. The girl who didn't take risks. Who didn't want to be watched. Who stayed two steps ahead of the curve because anything less felt like failure.

I preferred the sidelines and shadows. But for one night, it had felt... safe to want to be seen. Probably because of the mask. Why that gorgeous confection of sparkles and feathers felt like permission, I didn't know. But it did.

Or it had.

"But now the whole thing feels stupid," I whispered. "Like I was playing dress-up. Like I thought I could be that kind of girl for one night, and the universe reminded me—loudly—that I'm not."

Blair reached across the space between us and took my hand. "You don't need Jeff. You don't need anyone. You need to shine. You wanted that moment because you were ready to claim it. You still are. He doesn't get to take that from you. You don't need a date. Go as a goddess of vengeance. Let people worship you."

I snorted at the absurdity of the notion. "I don't think I have the energy to be worshipped."

Blair pointed to the dress. "You had the energy when you bought that."

I looked at the dress again, the way the fabric shimmered, unapologetic and powerful, and I felt the pinch of longing behind my breastbone. "But it doesn't feel the same."

"No," she agreed. "It feels better. Because now? Now it's not about him. It never should've been. This is your resurrection, babe."

The words landed like a chord I didn't know I'd been waiting to hear. Not a battle cry, but a benediction. I'd never walked into a room and felt beautiful. Not once in my life. I knew how to be smart, how to be prepared, how to win approval with a sharp retort or a solid résumé. I knew how to be impressive.

But I'd never known how to be seen.

"I don't want to do this to prove anything to him," I said finally, voice tight.

"Good." Blair's hand squeezed mine. "Then don't. Do it to prove something to yourself."

The silence that followed was thick and full and strangely calm. No pressure. No agenda. Just that glimmer of possibility that hadn't entirely gone out yet.

My fingers flexed around the cup. "Okay."

Blair's answering grin lit up the entire room like someone had flipped a switch. "There she is."

She popped up off the bed like she'd been waiting for this exact moment. "We've got lashes to prep, magic to conjure, and at least one goddess to resurrect." She placed the mask back in its velvet box like it was a royal crown and grabbed the dress from the closet hook with a reverence that almost made me laugh.

"Come on. We have two days to perfect this look. We're going back to my place. Better lighting, better mirror, and the glitter selection of your dreams."

Chapter 5

Ramsey

Bodie sat next to me, flipping a football between his hands like he needed the distraction as he watched some ESPN game rerun on the screen. But ever since Blair showed up, I'd struggled to focus. Not because Blair was a vortex of chaos energy, but because I was trying to hear her conversation with Alia. Or, more properly, trying to keep myself from trying to overhear their conversation and trying to hear it, anyway.

It was impossible not to catch... snippets.

Alia's voice barely registered—a low, quiet thread I couldn't make out. But Blair?

"You don't need a date." Her retort echoed sharp and bright. "Go as a goddess of vengeance. Let people worship you."

My jaw tightened.

Worship her?

Jesus. Don't go there, man.

But my brain didn't listen. It immediately offered up the image: Alia in that dress—the one I'd caught a glimpse of once when a delivery box had been opened in the wrong room. Dark purple, sleek and bold in a way that begged for a double take. Her hair pulled back. Her shoulders bare. That damn mask with the feathers and metallic edge catching the light while she looked at me like she already knew all my secrets.

Worship her? Yeah. That would be easy.

Too easy.

I shifted on the couch, grinding my molars together like that might force the thought back into whatever hole it crawled out of. Right next to me, Bodie didn't say a word. Which made me extra aware of how *right there* he was. How not okay it would be if he ever knew what I was thinking.

I dragged my focus back to the TV, like the scoreboard could erase what I'd just imagined.

Blair meant it as a joke—or actually, maybe not —but the idea of touching Alia, tasting her, had rewired my brain.

God help me.

Blair came striding down the hall like a woman on a mission, one arm looped around the dress and the velvet mask box tucked securely in the other. Alia trailed behind her, sweater sleeves pulled over her hands, hair slightly mussed like they'd already started planning something major.

She didn't look at me right away—but just before she crossed the threshold into the living room, her gaze flicked up. Met mine.

Not long. Maybe half a second. But it was enough.

There was something soft and steady in her eyes. A pulse of quiet steel under all the shit she was carrying. Like she wasn't just surviving it. She was choosing not to break.

My chest did something weird and traitorous.

"Emergency fashion summit." Blair tossed the words over her shoulder with trademark flair. "Don't wait up."

The door clicked shut behind them.

"She's still going to that thing?" Bodie muttered beside me, his voice tight.

I nodded, forcing my voice calm. "Looks like it."

And damn it, I was proud of her. After everything, after that asshole gutted her pride in public, she wasn't backing down. That took guts. Fire. But pride wasn't the only thing twisting in my ribs.

I was worried.

And underneath that—buried deep where it had no business being—was the raw, hungry want

I'd spent years trying to strangle quiet. The part of me that didn't want to keep my distance. That wanted to be the one walking in with her, matching tux and tie to her dress, her hand resting easy on my arm like she belonged there. With me.

Bodie didn't say anything right away, but I could feel the shift in him. His shoulders tensed, eyes narrowing like he was already running mental background checks on every guy who might be at that party. His jaw flexed. "Those parties are full of drunk frat guys and half-assed security."

Yeah. He was thinking the same thing I was.

Who was going to be watching her back?

Bodie scrubbed a hand over his face and sat forward, elbows on his knees. "I don't like her going alone."

I didn't answer right away. He wasn't wrong, but jumping in would blow up in our faces. Alia would take it like we didn't think she could take care of herself. Worse, we'd probably wreck whatever confidence she was just starting to get back after everything with Barrett the fuckwad.

I kept my voice even. "She can handle herself."

"She shouldn't have to!" Bodie scrubbed a hand down his face before continuing in a quieter tone. "That's not the point. It's not about her. It's about everyone else."

I watched him for a second, weighing the line

we were tiptoeing up to. He was worried, but not hovering. Not trying to control her. Just being the kind of brother who'd seen too many things go sideways and knew exactly what kind of entitled assholes showed up to parties like that.

I leaned back against the couch. "So, what are you suggesting?"

He turned toward me, jaw set. "We get into the party."

"It's a closed event," I pointed out, even though I already knew where this was going. "We're not frat guys. We're not dates. We're not even invited."

Bodie leaned back, arms crossing over his chest like I'd dared him to find a loophole. "It's a masquerade. You think they're doing facial recognition at the door?"

I gave him a flat look. "It's a formal masquerade. We're gonna stand out if we show up in jeans and attitude."

He shrugged, like that was barely a speed bump. "So we don't. We get tuxes."

I stared at him. "You make that sound like we've got them hanging in a closet somewhere."

"I've got a cousin who still owes me from that wedding he bailed on last summer. And you're roughly the same size."

I ran a hand over my jaw, feeling the edges of

my resistance starting to give. "Okay. And the masks?"

That grin spread over his face—mischief and determination all rolled into one. "You leave that to me."

Of course. I should've known. I suspected he'd go to exactly the same source Alia had used. And why wouldn't he? Gibson Hollow was only an hour and a half away. If anybody had the hookup, it would be Bodie's Uncle Dee.

Still, the weight in my chest hadn't gone anywhere. "I don't know about this, man." I looked toward the front door, where Alia had disappeared not five minutes ago. "I don't think she'd want us there."

"We're not gonna crash it." Bodie sat forward again. "We're not gonna interfere. Just shadows, that's it. Watch her back. Make sure she doesn't have to deal with some creep while she's trying to enjoy herself."

He said it like it was obvious. Like it was a mission.

And I hated how much I wanted to say yes.

I wanted to say it was about protection. That I only wanted to keep an eye out, play quiet backup in case the night threw her into the orbit of some beer-soaked asshole with zero respect for boundaries.

And, sure, that was part of it. But it wasn't the whole story.

The truth lodged sharp in my throat, unwanted and undeniable: I didn't want to be there just to keep her safe.

I wanted to see her.

In the dress. In the mask. In that glow I'd only caught glimpses of—never mine, never meant for me—but still enough to keep me hooked. I wanted to watch her walk into that ballroom like it belonged to her. Like she belonged there, not on the sidelines where the world always tried to tuck her.

She deserved her Cinderella moment, and I wanted to be the one at her side. Her arm looped through mine, her voice soft near my ear, her smile something I could steal without guilt.

But that wasn't on the table. Not with Bodie sitting five feet away. Not with the years between us and all the unspoken rules that came with them.

If I couldn't be the guy who got to worship her in the way Blair—loud and unrepentant—had thrown into the air like a dare, then maybe I could be the guy who made sure no one unworthy tried.

Even if it wrecked me a little.

I nodded once, leaned into the part of the truth I could say out loud.

"Fine." I blew out a slow breath. "But we stay

out of the way. If she catches us hovering, she'll kill us both."

Bodie didn't even blink. "Deal."

We bumped fists, quiet and sure, no victory whoops or posturing. Merely a silent agreement sealed in the space between worry and something like devotion.

Then I reached for my drink, took a long pull, and stared at the front door like I could still see her silhouette beyond it.

She had no idea we were coming.

And if we did it right, she never would.

Chapter 6

Alia

The night of the masquerade party, Blair had half my hair twisted into pin curls and a dozen open makeup palettes spread across her desk like some kind of Impressionist orgy when I finally let myself breathe.

Her apartment was warm with lamplight, music pulsing low, something upbeat and glittery, like it had just stepped out of a New York drag revue and wanted to take the world dancing. It suited her. It made me smile. The kind of real, down-in-my-bones smile that had felt rare lately. Uncle Dee would approve.

The smell of setting spray and setting powder mixed with the faint cinnamon of the tea she'd forced into my hand an hour ago. It felt like we were inside a snow globe—self-contained, still. Bodie hadn't said anything about tonight, but that didn't mean he didn't have thoughts. Twinsense didn't lie. He didn't approve. Not that he didn't think I could or should go out. He just worried. But he'd elected not to hover, and for that I was grateful. He'd texted this afternoon that he was taking the car, and I hadn't asked why.

Blair was doing me a solid, not only by being my own personal fairy godmother, but by loaning me her car, so I wouldn't be stranded if I wanted to leave at any point.

She tugged gently at a pinned curl. "You're not allowed to look until I'm done. No mirror cheating."

"Wasn't planning on it."

"Good. I want you to get the full effect. We're aiming for stunned silence followed by tears of joy."

I gave her a look. "I mean, maybe not tears. I don't want to undo all your hard work."

"Baby, this look will be going *nowhere* after I'm through with you." She grinned around the makeup brush she had between her teeth like a cigarette. Glitter shimmered on her cheekbone, a little transferred from me, but more from her own canvas. Blair was always a few degrees more than reality could handle. It wasn't just the highlighter or the statement lipstick she'd already picked out. It was the way she moved—sharp and precise and proud. Her femininity was a declaration, not a disguise.

And she'd earned every inch of it.

I didn't say that. I just let her keep working, the brush sweeping soft against my skin, cool fingers shifting my jaw into the right angles.

"You've been quiet," she said after a while, softer now.

I shrugged. "Just tired."

She made a noncommittal sound. Not pushing, not pressing. But I could feel the question hanging there, anyway.

I didn't have a good answer. I didn't feel nervous, exactly. Not anymore. That emotion had long since calcified into something more complicated.

Because this wasn't really about Jeff. It hadn't been for days. It was about the way everyone looked at me with pity or uncertainty, like I might break if they said the wrong thing. As if getting dumped had turned me from competent to fragile overnight. I hated it. Hated that walking into this party would feel like walking into a courtroom where everyone already thought they knew the story.

And yet... I still wanted to go.

Not to prove anything to anyone. Not even him. But because I'd wanted this night before it all fell apart. Because I'd paid for that dress with my own damn time and effort, and I'd earned the right to wear it. Because wanting something just for me didn't make me selfish.

I was tired of folding in on myself.

And tonight, I didn't have to.

My phone buzzed where it sat on the corner of the desk, half-buried under a tangle of bobby pins and a tube of something called "Radiance Primer."

Blair didn't notice. She was too busy muttering to herself about eyeshadow pigment and the cowardice of cheap brushes. I wiped my hand on my leg and reached for the phone.

TESS:

Hey! I just heard from Daniel and thought you should know—Jeff is planning to come tonight. Apparently, he's bringing a date. Just wanted to give you a heads-up, in case that affects your plans 🤍

For a second, I just stared at the screen. The words didn't land all at once. They slid in sideways, like cold water under a door. I didn't even realize I was holding my breath until the room tilted.

And there it was. Not heartbreak. Not even anger. Just... dread.

Everyone would know. Everyone would be watching. Not because they cared about me, but because a story like this begged for an ending, and nothing said "drama" like your ex showing up with a replacement while you stood there alone in heels and pride.

I wasn't stupid. I'd seen the glances all week at the sorority house. The conversations that stopped just a little too fast when I walked in. The sympathy in people's eyes that felt like someone pressing on a bruise just to see if it still hurt.

And now? Now I was walking into a powder keg with a lit match and a purple dress.

The anxiety set in like static, low and crawling. A quiet simmer that made me want to pull into myself.

I didn't care about Jeff. God, I really didn't. But I hated the idea of him becoming the lens everyone viewed me through. I hated that the narrative would always circle back to that night. To me watching him kiss someone else while I stood in a bar, trying not to cry in front of friends and strangers.

The worst part wasn't what he'd done. It was what it echoed. The fear that maybe I wasn't enough. That wanting something for myself had been foolish. That this whole thing—this night, this dress, this mask—wasn't reclamation.

It was desperation.

And now everyone would see it.

I stared at the text until the screen dimmed, my reflection faint in the black glass. Mouth bare. Eyes shadowed. Half-finished.

"Hey." Blair's voice cut through the buzz in my head, sharper now. She must've seen my face. "What just happened?"

My fingers curled around the phone. I didn't look at her. Not yet.

"He's coming tonight." My voice barely made it out of my throat. "With a date."

The words hung there like smoke. I didn't look at Blair. Couldn't. I just stared at the middle distance like maybe the air could unravel the knot twisting in my gut.

"I don't want to walk into that room and feel like a cautionary tale."

Blair said nothing, but I felt her stillness behind me. All that glittering energy gone taut.

"I don't want their pity." The words tumbled out faster now. "I can't stand the way they look at me. Like I'm some wounded little duck who needs to be protected from big, bad heartbreak." I made a scoffing sound that didn't quite qualify as a laugh. "It's not even about him anymore. Not really. It's about what he took."

My hands curled into frustrated fists. "This was supposed to be *my* night. And now it's gonna be his. Again."

For a heartbeat, Blair didn't move. Then she straightened to her full height like a queen donning her crown, all softness replaced with fire. "First of all, he doesn't get to hijack your night. Not unless you hand it to him."

She stepped closer, eyeliner immaculate, energy coiled like a storm barely held in check. "Second of all, you are not the girl who gets pitied. You are the girl who walks into a room and makes people regret underestimating her. And if they don't see that the second you step through the door? Make. Them. Look."

I blinked, but she wasn't finished. Not even close.

"This isn't about him. It never was. This is about you. Reclaiming your space. Daring them to look and not blink. And if they pity you?" She tilted her head, smile almost sharklike in its fierceness. "That's because they don't know what power looks like when it's aimed straight at their throats."

And then the final blow, spoken so softly it hit like a sledgehammer. "You said you didn't want to feel invisible anymore. So don't. Make them see you. Make him wish he'd never been so fucking stupid as to take you for granted."

The silence that followed wasn't empty. It was full of something sharp and electric. Like a fuse had been lit, and all I had to do was decide whether to let it burn.

I didn't say anything at first. Just breathed. Let the silence wrap around me like gauze, thin and fragile, but holding everything in.

Then I nodded.

Blair didn't cheer. Didn't beam. She just exhaled like she'd known I'd get here all along. Then she moved with practiced grace. The dress came off its hanger, flowing like liquid midnight in her arms as she handed it to me. "Time to suit up, buttercup."

She turned away, not because she was modest, but because she knew I needed the space. I stepped into the dress slowly, reverently, like every inch of fabric meant something. And it did. It was a promise I'd made to myself, long before Jeff ever touched my life. Blaire was right: this was never about him.

Zipping the back, I felt the fabric hug my waist, settle against my ribs, cascade over my hips like it had been stitched to remind me that I had always, always been allowed to want something for myself.

I stepped into the heels—high, silver, and unapologetically bold.

Blair returned to my side like a general before battle. She reached into her makeup bag, pulled out the lipstick tube labeled "Hex," and held it between two fingers like it was sacred.

She uncapped it with a click that sounded far louder than it should have. "I wore this the night I came out to my family. They didn't all take it well. But I did it anyway. Because some truths don't need permission."

She turned to me. "Your turn."

I tilted my chin.

She swiped the color onto my lips with a precision that felt ceremonial. The deep berry red gleamed like lacquered armor.

"Let him choke on it," Blair murmured.

And then came the final piece. She opened the velvet box, pulled out the mask, and held it up like a coronation. "You ready?"

I took it from her hands. The feathers swept upward like wings, the metallic accents catching the bedroom light. When I settled it onto my face and tied the satin ribbons behind my head, something clicked into place. Not transformation, not pretend, but alignment.

I looked at my reflection in the mirror. The purple of the dress shimmered like the first light of dawn, catching lines I hadn't admired before: the curve of my neck, the subtle strength in my shoulders, the way the fabric hugged my ribs without asking permission. Each detail of the mask, the heels, the lipstick—they weren't a costume. They were declarations, pieces of armor forged from intention rather than guilt.

I traced the mask's feathers with a gentle fingertip as if they carried their own breath. The metallic edge of the mask caught the lamp's glow and sharpened my cheekbones, gave me posture I didn't know I'd lost. In that moment, I wasn't someone trying to be seen—I was simply visible. Unburied. Entirely me.

There was a thrill in my chest when I realized this wasn't a transformation so much as a homecoming. A quiet bloom of something powerful, claiming space I typically shrank from. This was the mirror finally catching up with all the years I lived in preparation, waiting for the applause. Now, the mirror offered witness.

My breath settled slow. The night ahead wasn't about revenge or proving people wrong. It was proof I'd already chosen myself. I inhaled deep, feeling the sturdy lift of the dress around my waist and the cool slide of satin ribbons at my neck. This was reclamation felt in skin and bone and stance.

I didn't need to become someone else. I just needed to step into who I'd always been beneath the surface. And damn it, I looked ready.

Blair stepped up behind me, catching my gaze in the mirror as she laid a hand on my shoulder.

I reached up to cover her hand with mine. "Thank you. For this. For everything."

Her mouth curved—not into a smirk or a grin, but something gentler. Fiercer. "You didn't need me, babe. You just needed reminding."

I nodded, eyes stinging. "Still. Thank you."

Blair squeezed my shoulder. "Go give 'em whiplash."

I turned to the door, grabbed my small clutch, and let out one long breath. This wasn't the safe choice. It wasn't the quiet one. But for once, that wasn't the point.

I didn't have an entourage. I didn't have a plan. But I had steel in my spine and war paint on my lips. I stepped out into the night—alone, but not lonely.

And this time, I didn't shrink from the world. I walked straight into it.

Chapter 7

Ramsey

BODIE:

> Rick's girl rear-ended a parked car. Might be a concussion. ER run just in case. I'm taking him. Go without me. She's less likely to clock you, anyway.

Classic twinsense logic. We'd talked before about how Bodie thought Alia might know he was there as soon as she walked in the room. But me? I was background noise.

Yeah, that's not sus at all. I'm one hundred per-cent checking in with Rick later to see if this ER run really happened.

I squinted into the passenger-side mirror of my

beat-up truck, trying to straighten a crooked tie that wasn't even mine, tugged the mask down from my forehead and settled it over my face. Took a deep breath like I was about to step onto the field wondering—for the millionth time—if this was a bad idea. The last thing I wanted to do was get in Alia's way tonight, piss her off, make her feel like she couldn't stand on her own.

But staying away hadn't felt right either. Not when I knew what kind of night she was walking into. Not when I knew how hard she'd fought just to put that dress on.

The tux sleeves tugged at my shoulders, tight enough to remind me this wasn't tailored. Hell, the whole outfit had come from Bodie's cousin, who wore his muscle mass like decoration instead of profession. And I was about to go sneak through a back door like I was pulling a heist instead of crashing a glorified frat party.

Which... okay. Maybe a little of both.

The venue was one of those multipurpose halls the university used for everything from parties to alumni donor dinners. I skirted the side of the building, avoiding the main entrance, and slipped in through a cracked service door at the back. It closed behind me with a soft click that still sounded too loud. A couple of catering staff gave me a glance but didn't stop me. Apparently, being massive and in a tux was enough to pass.

I moved fast. My nerves had me on edge, adrenaline buzzing under my skin like I was walking into a fight I didn't know the rules for. I told myself I was here to check on her. Keep watch from a distance. Let her have her night. But that wasn't the whole truth, and I knew it.

I wanted to see her. Just her.

It was ridiculous, really, trying to act like a shadow when I was built like a walk-in freezer. The narrow service hallway felt like it shrank around me with every step. I dodged a tower of champagne flutes, ducked under a hanging exit sign, and tried to ignore the very real possibility that I was about to get kicked out for impersonating an invited guest because I had to see her.

Not talk. Not interfere. Just... see.

See if she was okay. See if she'd really done it—put on the dress, the mask, stepped into that room like she owned it. Like she was done hiding.

The hallway spit me out behind a curtain near what I guessed was the DJ booth—currently occupied by some guy in a gold half-mask and a bomber jacket, bobbing his head to a remix of something that might've been Rihanna. Or maybe Beyoncé. It was hard to tell under the bass line rattling the windows.

The venue itself had clearly started out classy—arched doorways, polished floors, string lights dripping from beams overhead. Gilded wall sconces and some heavy velvet curtains tried to pretend this was high society. But the illusion crumbled fast under the strobe lights and the swarm of college students moving like a single drunken organism. Obviously, a bunch of them had pre-gamed before the party.

People were everywhere. Twirling, shouting, half-dancing, half-grinding to the beat. Costumes ranged from elegant to absurd—lace ballgowns paired with feathered masks and Converse sneakers, full tuxedos undone at the neck, a pair of guys in matching vampire capes tossing ping-pong balls into plastic cups at a side table like this was still a frat house.

I adjusted my mask and moved fast, keeping to the edges, trying not to get caught in anyone's orbit. No one paid me much attention. There was too much noise, too many distractions. Only one more guy in a monkey suit.

But even in all the chaos, my guard stayed up as I continued scanning the room.

Will I even recognize her?

It was a stupid question. Alia could be wearing a wig and head-to-toe sequins, and I'd still know her walk. The tilt of her chin. The way she moved when she didn't think anyone was watching.

The crowd pulsed again as the music shifted, and for a split second I let the doubt creep in. What if I couldn't find her? What if she didn't want to be found?

My fingers curled into fists at my sides, the fabric of the tux straining against my shoulders as I kept weaving through the bodies and noise. The plan was simple: get in, keep my distance, make sure she was okay, and that she stayed that way.

Simple.

Except nothing about this felt simple now. Not when I was desperate to see her step into that spotlight. For once, I wanted to witness what she looked like when she didn't hold anything back.

I turned from the punch table, pretending to be fascinated by the label on a half-empty bottle of off-brand sparkling cider, and nearly crashed straight into her.

I stopped short, one step away from repeating the moment I hadn't been able to shake since Whiskey Jack's—the jolt of collision, the feel of her arms in mine, the look on her face when her world had split in half.

Only... this wasn't that night. She wasn't running. She wasn't devastated. She was standing tall. Shoulders back. Chin lifted like she owned the goddamn room.

And maybe she did.

The dress was purple. Not soft or sweet or forgettable, but deep, dangerous, and dramatic. There was probably some fancy girl name for the shade of it. All I could call it was stunning. It clung to her like it had been sewn straight onto her skin, dipping at the back, slit at the thigh, daring you to keep your eyes up. Her heels added inches to her already-perfect posture, and every precise and deliberate step she took struck like punctuation. A rhythm she set, and the room followed. Because the other people in the room definitely noticed her.

And I couldn't blame them.

I'd seen her angry. I'd seen her focused, tired, laughing so hard she snorted soda out her nose—but this? This was different. This was deliberate. She'd chosen to be seen tonight. Chosen power, precision, boldness. And I was so far gone I didn't know whether I wanted to shield her or drop to one knee and vow allegiance.

Her mask was black and metallic purple, with silver accents. Intricate, with a subtle gleam that caught the lights enough to hint at something wicked. Feathers curled from both sides, not overdone—flirting with the edge of mystery. The whole thing had been made to flaunt those long-lashed eyes of hers. The eyes that slid up to mine and made the whole damn room fall away for a second.

It didn't matter that half her face was hidden. That she hadn't said a word. I knew.

Of course I knew.

The way she stood. The shape of her mouth. The fire in the set of her shoulders. It wasn't just recognition—it was something lower and deeper. Like gravity shifted, and every part of me aligned toward her without needing to think about it.

And underneath that pull was a flicker of something rawer. Pride maybe. Or awe. Or that selfish little corner of me that wanted to believe she looked this powerful, this untouchable, because she'd finally stopped shrinking for people who didn't deserve her.

She held my gaze. Not startled, not shy. Her expression didn't shift. There was no gasp of recognition, no subtle tilt that said she knew what I was hiding beneath the mask.

Which meant maybe she didn't know it was me. Not for sure.

And God help me, maybe that was safer, because I didn't trust myself to speak. I didn't trust myself not to give everything away. This version of her—standing fully in her power, beautiful and unapologetic—made it that much harder to remember all the reasons I couldn't reach for more.

My hands hovered for a breath before I realized they'd already moved—palms out, half-lifted in case

I needed to steady her. I didn't. She didn't stumble. Only slowed and stood her ground like a queen surveying the map before battle.

Then someone else moved into her orbit. Too slick. Too sure of himself. The kind of guy who treated his reflection like a second date. Tux sharp, hair sharper, mask probably custom. I could smell the cologne from ten feet away. The way he angled in beside her was pure calculation. Not hello. Not can I join you? Assumption that he could and would be welcomed.

His hand lightly skimmed her elbow, like maybe he thought that made it okay. She shifted a half step back, polite, but firm. Drawing a line he pretended not to see.

I didn't think. Didn't hesitate. One step, and I was there, slipping into the space at her side like I'd always been meant to fill it. I didn't touch her at first. I let the size of me speak before anything else did. Then, with deliberate calm, I dropped my hand to the small of her back.

"There you are. Been looking everywhere for you."

She didn't blow the cover. She simply looked up at me through that razor-edged mask, like this was exactly where I was supposed to be.

And for one breathless second, I wondered if she knew. If the weight of that look was something more. There was something in the way she held my gaze—steady, almost familiar. A little too familiar?

But then she didn't say my name. Didn't blink like she recognized the guy behind the voice. Her expression stayed level, unreadable in a way that made it easier to breathe.

That was all I needed.

I shifted closer. Not crowding her, but making sure there was no space for slick-boy to pretend he hadn't been dismissed.

The guy blinked. Straightened his cuffs like maybe that would salvage his ego. "Didn't realize you were with someone."

"We're good now." I didn't smile. Didn't offer an out. I stood there, a wall with a voice, waiting for him to go.

He held my gaze one second too long before muttering something and turning away.

I didn't watch him go. I was too aware of the girl beside me, the heat of her body through the thin fabric between us, the way her breathing didn't waver.

She looked up at me, one brow arched beneath the gleam of her mask. The corner of her mouth tugged like she was trying not to laugh. "I had that handled."

I lifted my hands in surrender. "I know. Didn't mean to interfere."

That was a lie. I'd absolutely meant to interfere. But I hadn't meant to get caught wanting to.

"Just..." I shrugged, stepping back a little. Giving her space. "Guys like that tend not to take no for an answer. Figured it wouldn't hurt to make things clear."

Her gaze lingered a second longer, like she was deciding how to take that. There was a flicker of curiosity in her eyes. Not suspicious, exactly, but... like she was trying to place me. Then she nodded, once. A subtle acknowledgment. A silent thank-you, maybe.

I glanced around, trying to remember what the hell I was supposed to be doing. Watching. Protecting. Blending in. None of that felt right anymore.

"Need help finding your date?" I kept my voice neutral.

She tilted her head. "Don't have one."

I'd known that. It was the whole reason Bodie had come up with this lunatic scheme in the first place. But the words still hit me like a delayed punch to the chest. I managed a casual nod, like the idea of her being free at last didn't give me all kinds of... notions. I couldn't see her whole face, but I could see her mouth. And right now, it was unreadable.

The charged silence stretched.

This wasn't part of the plan. I wasn't supposed to engage. I wasn't supposed to want.

But I did.

And apparently, I was an idiot.

I cleared my throat, nerves pricking under my collar. "Me neither. You wanna..." I faltered. Damn it. Why was this suddenly the hardest thing I'd ever done? "You wanna hang out?"

Hang out? Jesus. What was I, fourteen?

But instead of giving that the laugh or scoff it deserved, she flashed a warm smile that was bright enough to kick my pulse into overdrive. "Yeah. I think I'd like that."

The whole damn world tilted. I did my best to hold back a grin and a fist pump. "Should we introduce ourselves?" The words slipped out before I could think better of them.

Abort! Abort! This wasn't the plan! She's not supposed to know it's you.

But she didn't flinch. Didn't blink like she recognized me as anything more than a stranger in a mask. Amusement curved her lips. "I think the entire point of this kind of party is the mystery."

Look at her, saving me from myself.

If she'd known—really known—it would've shown. Wouldn't it? She would've tilted her head just a little differently. Said my name. Asked why I was here. Something. But she hadn't. And now she was giving me this moment, like it meant nothing more than what it was.

So maybe she didn't know.

And maybe that was okay.

I didn't have to explain. Didn't have to ruin it with reality. I could just... be here. With her. For a little while.

She didn't say anything else. Only turned slightly, that deep purple dress catching the light like smoke over a flame, and offered the barest tip of her head in invitation.

I stepped into stride beside her.

Not as Ramsey. Not as Bodie's best friend or the guy she probably thought she'd never see like this. Not as the person who'd walked her home that night without ever saying the words he shouldn't say.

Just a man behind a mask.

And she was nobody's sister, nobody's ex. Not tonight. Tonight, she was a mystery in purple and shadow, her name swallowed by the bass line, and her intentions lost somewhere in the curve of her smile.

Some part of me—maybe the last sane one— whispered that this was dangerous. That the more I leaned into the game, the harder it would be to let go.

But I didn't stop.

Because this was the only version of the story where I got to stand beside her like this, unburdened by all the reasons I shouldn't. This was the loophole in the contract. The space between the lines.

Behind the mask, I could pretend.

And for one night, I was going to let myself believe I had the right to want her.

So I didn't walk away.

Chapter 8

Alia

We'd been orbiting each other for hours. Circulating. Talking. Laughing more than I expected—about nothing that mattered and everything that somehow did. Never names. Never anything that would strip away the mask. That was the rule. Or maybe the unspoken understanding between two people pretending this wasn't what it was.

I knew it was Ramsey. I'd known since the moment we nearly collided. You didn't mistake a man built like a battering ram. And I knew those eyes. I'd had three years to learn what they looked like when they were watching out for someone. For me.

Bodie had sent him. I knew my twin. Understood that he hadn't wanted me to be here alone—

and that he also knew I'd have been livid if he'd shown up to be bodyguard himself. These past hours wouldn't have been nearly as much fun without Ramsey by my side, so rather than be annoyed at Bodie's high handedness, I was touched and grateful that he'd thought of this. And, for a while, I'd told myself that was all it was. Big brother orders, protective best friend execution. But the longer the night wore on, the less that explanation held. Ramsey wasn't simply circling like a bodyguard. He was staying close because he wanted to. Because this meant something—to him. To me.

It was dangerous territory. And I didn't care.

So when the crowd surged, I didn't resist it. Someone bumped me from behind, and I stumbled a step closer to him, heels catching against the scuffed dance floor. His hand was already there, steadying me before I could catch myself. Callused fingers curling below my elbow and sending sparks up my arm.

The music shifted again, slow and sweet this time. Alison Krauss, soft and aching, her voice curling through the air like something private that wasn't meant to be overheard. The kind of song that made the whole room feel smaller, quieter, as if everyone had taken one collective breath and was holding it. Fiddles laced under the melody like a heartbeat—that soft southern ache that made it impossible to pretend this wasn't about something real.

He turned to face me fully and offered his hand. A question in the shape of an open palm.

I took it. Because why not? Because I wanted to. Because, for the first time in... God, maybe ever, I wasn't being anyone's daughter or sister or backup plan. I wasn't calculating or caretaking. I was only me. Wanting something for no other reason than the fact that I wanted it.

My fingers slid into his, and the contact sent a thrill up my arm.

He didn't say anything. Neither did I. But when he pulled me gently into the middle of the floor, every part of me went electric. His hand found the curve of my waist like it belonged there. A steady, warm assurance that he had me.

Our other hands met in the space between us. His fingers wrapping around mine in a way that felt more like a promise than a step in a dance. And still, neither of us spoke. There was no need.

He didn't move like a guy at a college party—jerky or ironic or trying too hard. He moved like a man tuned in. His lead was gentle but intentional, and my body followed without hesitation. Because of course it did. Because it always had. Because something in me never stopped listening for the way he moved.

And then, as we turned in a slow, weightless pivot like the world had softened just for us, he leaned in. Close enough to find the space beside my ear, where his breath could skate across my skin like a spark. "Do you always lead?"

The murmured words lit something inside me—sharp and playful and way too close to dangerous.

"Only when someone lets me." I tilted my head so the words whispered against his jaw, darkened by the faint rasp of stubble. I wondered what he'd taste like there.

His laugh was a low rumble, more felt than heard. It rippled through my hand on his chest, down my spine to settle somewhere low and aching. And in that moment, it didn't matter that this was stupid, or risky, or entirely unsustainable. All that mattered was the way I was standing in the center of a crowd and still somehow felt like the only girl in the room.

The mask was saving me. If I had to acknowledge who he was, who I was, I'd get nervous and fumble everything. My crush would come out, and then I'd never be able to look him in the eye again until we graduated and went our separate ways. But this way? This way I could be bold. I could flirt. I could let myself want without consequence. Because this wasn't real, right? This was masquerade magic. Fantasy. A loophole in the rules.

His hand shifted a few inches higher on my back. Not bold or groping. Just... attentive. As if he was giving me the chance to step away or say this was too much.

I didn't. Instead, I leaned in. And maybe that was nothing. A line in the air. A slight change to the music. But my pulse was thunder in my ears. My breath came tight and shallow. My whole body was humming, strung so taut I could barely stand it. Because this wasn't a game anymore. Not really. And if I let myself believe this was pretend... I could survive it. At least until the music stopped.

He pulled back to look at me again. Not because the song had ended or because the moment had passed. But to *look* at me. To really see me.

And he did.

Not in the way guys usually looked. Not like he was trying to peel me apart with his eyes or figure out how far he could get before the mask slipped. He looked like he was memorizing. Like this—this dance, this moment, this version of me I barely recognized but desperately wanted to be—was something worth keeping.

And I hated how much I liked that. How much I needed it.

No one ever really saw me. Not unless I was fighting. Not unless I was proving I was the smartest person in the room or the one most likely to make sure everything didn't fall apart. But this? This wasn't about proving anything. And still, he looked at me like I mattered. Like I was enough, even now—especially now—standing in the middle of a crowd in female war paint and a mask, trying to remember how to breathe.

I arched a brow, trying for light. "What?"

His gaze didn't waver. "Nothing." Soft. Solid. Like the word had weight.

But it wasn't nothing. We both knew that.

It was everything.

I didn't see it coming. Not exactly. There was no dramatic pause, no shift in music to signal something was about to change. Merely the same quiet ache winding through the melody, the same soft press of his hand at my back, the same steady presence of him, holding the world still around us.

We weren't alone. Not even close. There were bodies on all sides, voices and footsteps and perfume and too much men's body spray, but it all blurred into background noise. For one suspended second, it felt as if the rest of the room slipped away. Like we'd fallen between the cracks of reality and found a space that belonged only to us.

His hand lifted, slow and cautious, and I felt the brush of his knuckles along my cheek. A barely there question that electrified every nerve ending. I didn't answer with words. I stayed right where I was, let the space between us stay small, let the silence speak for me as I turned the barest fraction into the touch. I wanted this. Wanted him almost more than my next breath.

Heart thundering, I watched him slowly close the distance, dipping his head toward mine. He hesitated a fraction of an inch away. Not changing his mind, but giving me the choice. I didn't think. Couldn't. I simply lifted my mouth to his as if drawn by a gravitational force. And maybe I was. Three years of silently crushing on this man. Three years of shoving down those feelings. Of comparing every guy I dated to him and finding them lacking.

His lips brushed mine, an unbearably tender caress that melted every atom of good sense and set me on fire. I felt drunk and dazzled all at once. It wasn't sweet. It was earth shattering, life altering devastation. And I was so here for every second.

Something inside me broke loose, a deep, secret, reckless part that pressed closer to the heat of him, flattening my palm against his chest, feeling the solid, muscled shape of him beneath the tux. One of his hands curved at the back of my neck, cupping my nape. As much an anchor as a claiming, and everything in me sparked like fireworks.

Oh God, this was going to ruin me. And I didn't think I cared. I just didn't want this exquisite moment to end. Didn't want to lose the taste of him against my tongue, the feel of his body, warm and perfect, still swaying with mine in time to the music. Because it wasn't simply good. It was everything. Everything I hadn't let myself want, everything I'd tried to tuck away. And now it was here, *actually* happening, and I didn't know how to hold everything rioting inside me.

When he finally eased away, his lips left mine by slow degrees, as if he was still deciding whether to stay. His brow pressed gently against mine, and the weight of that simple touch nearly undid me all over again.

Neither of us spoke. Because saying anything would've cracked the moment wide open, and I wasn't ready to lose it. Not yet.

The song ended.

Or maybe it didn't. Maybe it bled into the next track without warning, the fiddles giving way to a driving beat and the low thrum of synth and bass. Around us, the crowd surged back to life—more bodies, more noise, more motion. The spell should've broken.

But he didn't move.

And neither did I.

We stayed exactly where we were, foreheads barely touching, his hand still warm at my back, mine curled loosely in his. Not swaying. Not talking. Each of us holding still in the eye of whatever this was. The air between us still felt thick with something that hadn't fully settled. My lips tingled. My skin buzzed. My thoughts were a messy tangle of breathless wonder and absolute disbelief.

I didn't know what happened next.

Didn't know if we stepped back into the masquerade and pretended none of this had happened. Didn't know if we kept pretending not to know who we were beneath the masks. If we danced again, or walked off, or simply let this night fold back into the version of our lives where he was my brother's best friend, and I was untouchable.

All I knew was—I wanted more.

I wasn't asking for a fairytale or forever. Simply more of this. More of him. The way he looked at me like I mattered. The way his touch made my body come alive. The way kissing him hadn't been terrifying or awkward or regrettable—it had been inevitable.

And maybe, just maybe, I was allowed to want that.

I felt the smile start behind my mask before I realized it was happening. Not a polite party smile. Not the charming one I wore when I was being the girl everyone expected. This one was stupid and giddy and so full of possibility it could barely fit in my chest.

He finally pulled back enough to look at me

again, eyes searching mine like he could hear every thought crashing around inside my skull.

I didn't say a word.

For now, the music was different. The night had changed. The world had tilted. And I was still standing. And as his own lips curved in return, I was maybe even starting to hope.

Chapter 9

Ramsey

The world hadn't quite restarted yet.

Alia was still close, her hand warm and steady over the center of my chest like she could anchor me there with just her touch. I didn't move. Didn't breathe. I wasn't sure I remembered how.

Everything inside me was buzzing, not like adrenaline from a game or the crackle of a fight about to break loose, but something deeper. More dangerous. Like I'd just crossed some invisible line, stepped off the edge of reason and landed somewhere I wasn't supposed to be—and found out it felt like heaven.

I'd kissed her. And she'd kissed me back. I hadn't imagined the way her body leaned into mine or the way her breath had caught or the soft, stunned sound she'd made, like maybe she'd been waiting for this just as long as I had.

I should've been thinking about Bodie and the fallout. About the impossibility of this actually working. About everything I'd just risked for five minutes of borrowed magic.

But the only thing circling in a relentless loop through my brain was how much I didn't want this to end. Not the night. Not the moment. Not her.

I wanted more. God help me, I wanted. And for once, I wasn't pretending otherwise.

For a flickering second, it didn't feel like a random Saturday night. It felt like New Year's. A beginning. Like a door swinging open to something I hadn't dared to name before now. She was still close, and I could feel her breath warm against my neck. I could still taste her—sweet and impossible. Everything inside me was thrumming like a struck chord, all shimmer and tension, like I'd just broken a rule and found heaven waiting on the other side.

I wanted to tell her. God, I wanted to *tell her*.

Rip off the mask, say, *It's me. I'm yours, if you'll have me.*

No more pretending. Just the bald-faced truth and all the risk that came with it. The words were right there. My mouth was already halfway open, the truth about to spill out and crack this whole night wide open.

Then my phone buzzed in my pocket. One long, low vibration, insistent enough to pull me back into my skin.

I hesitated, not wanting to look. Not wanting this spell to break. But what if it was Bodie? What if something had gone wrong? With an apologetic glance, I gave her fingers a quick, reassuring squeeze and shifted back enough to pull the phone out and check the screen.

The message lit up in blue and white.

COACH LANGSTON:

Johnston's out with a concussion. You're on the shortlist for the Charlotte Combine. Van leaves at 3 a.m. Be at the field house. No excuses.

For a second, I just stared at it. The words didn't make sense. Couldn't make sense. Not here, not now. Not when I was still standing in the after-glow of the best kiss of my life.

But they were real. They didn't go away when I blinked.

Johnston's out with a concussion.

Apparently that ER run Bodie mentioned had been the real deal.

The Charlotte Combine.

It wasn't just a tryout—it was *the* tryout. A high-profile regional showcase, sponsored by pro recruiters and stacked with NFL scouts. These things weren't open calls. You didn't just walk in and sign up. You were invited. Vetted. Plucked out of obscurity and offered the kind of spotlight that could rewrite your future.

And I'd just been offered a place because of Rick's shit luck.

This was the thing I'd trained for since my first year of high school. Every early morning lift, every brutal practice, every hit I'd taken and gotten back up from. The thing my mom had sacrificed for, working multiple jobs to pay for gear and training camps, because I had a dream and she believed in me. It all led here. This wasn't just a door opening. It was a rocket ignition.

And it meant leaving.

Right now.

No time to explain. No time to say what I really wanted to say. Just one choice in front of me—and it was the one I'd sworn I would never miss, not for anything.

Even if "anything" was standing inches away from me, her hand still holding mine.

I stared at the screen like maybe, if I waited long enough, it would change. Like maybe the words would vanish, or get rescinded, or turn out to be some elaborate mistake. But they didn't. They stayed, cold and final.

Part of me wanted to pocket the phone, say screw it, and lose myself in one more song. One more moment. One more breath with her close enough to taste. But the rest of me—the part that knew how few chances guys like me got—understood the truth:

If I didn't leave now, I wasn't going to leave at all.

And I couldn't blow this shot. Not even for her.

God, that hurt.

I turned back, and she was already watching me, her expression quiet and open and soft enough to ruin me. Like she knew something had shifted but wasn't going to ask. Like she trusted me to decide what happened next.

The words caught in my throat, thick and reluctant. "I have to go," I said finally, voice low.

A beat passed. My chest tightened. "I'm sorry."

Her expression didn't change, not exactly. But there was something in the way her mouth tilted, like she understood more than I was saying. Maybe more than I knew how to say.

I managed a crooked smile—aching and stupid

and real. "Don't forget me, mystery girl." But what I meant was: *Don't forget it's me.*

She didn't ask. Didn't press for some explanation as to why I was bolting like *I* was Cinderella at the ball and the clock had just struck midnight. Just looked at me, steady and sure, like she already knew everything I wasn't saying. Like maybe she'd known it all along.

"Impossible." Her voice was soft. Not some flirty brush-off, but a truth she was handing me to hold.

And God, it wrecked me. Not because it was too much. But because it was exactly what I wanted. Because she believed it. Because somewhere deep down, so did I.

I squeezed her hand, started to turn away—then stopped.

It was late. Past midnight now, and the party had shifted into that messier, looser kind of chaos that came when the cheap alcohol started running the show. Voices were louder, bodies closer, intentions murkier. The room felt different. Less golden. More unpredictable. And she was still standing in the middle of it all like some unclaimed flame, too steady, too good to be left alone in a crowd that didn't deserve her.

I realized I had no idea how she'd gotten here. "Can I give you a ride home?"

It would blow the illusion we were operating under, but damned if I was going to leave her on her own.

She didn't bristle or wave me off like I was being overprotective. She just smiled up at me. "I can drive myself. But you can walk me to my car."

I nodded, offering my arm. She took it without hesitation, her fingers curling lightly around my biceps like we'd done this a hundred times before.

We slipped back through the crowd together, the press of people parting just enough around us. I kept her close—half a step ahead, like I could shield her from the worst of it—and soaked in every second. The slide of her arm against mine. The brush of her dress when we shifted. The quiet ease between us that hadn't existed before tonight.

Outside, the air was cooler, clearer. The music still pulsed faintly from inside, but it felt like we'd stepped into a different world entirely. Quieter. Still.

We didn't speak, and I didn't know what I was going to say when we got to the car. I only knew I wasn't ready for this to be over.

So I walked slow. Let the silence stretch. Let myself look over at her and memorize the shape of her profile under the streetlight, the way her mask glinted when she turned her head, the way her fingers stayed curled in the crook of my arm like she didn't want to let go either.

For one night, I'd stood beside her. Danced with her. Kissed her. Held something fragile and impossible and too good to last.

But I had this walk. I had these last few minutes.

And I wasn't letting go until I had to.

Chapter 10

Alia

Outside, the air was cool against my flushed skin, the kind of night that smelled like autumn and felt like memory. His arm was steady under my hand as we slowly descended the stairs, like neither of us wanted to reach the bottom. The fabric of his jacket brushed against me with every step, warm and solid and far too easy to lean into.

I wasn't ready for this to be over.

The walk across the lot felt short and long at the same time. I led him to Blair's slightly beat-up RAV-4 parked under a lamppost and fished the keys from my clutch with fingers that weren't quite steady.

He stopped beside me. We didn't speak. Just

looked at each other across the narrow space between us, masks still on, like they could somehow hold back the tide of everything that wanted to spill out. My chest ached with the weight of what I wouldn't let myself ask for. What I didn't dare believe.

He shifted first. "I'm sorry." It sounded like it hurt to admit it. "I wish I didn't have to leave."

My heart squeezed. "It's okay." Somehow, I kept my voice steady. "You made my night. Thank you for that."

I didn't want to think about how it would've gone without him.

Another silence, this one thick with all the things we weren't saying. His gaze swept over my face, searching.

He took one step closer, his hands lifting as if he wanted to touch me. Then he stopped himself. "Can I—"

"God, yes."

And then he was kissing me again.

This time, it wasn't gentle. It wasn't sweet.

It was heat and hunger and everything we hadn't dared to reach for until now—every moment we'd danced around what simmered between us, every glance too long, every brush of hands that lingered just a second more than it should have. His hands found my waist, curving like they'd been made to hold me, and mine curled into the lapels of his jacket like I was afraid he might disappear if I let go.

The world tilted, just a little. Like something had unmoored and started spinning off its axis. Not wildly. Just enough to remind me that nothing would be the same after this.

The kiss wasn't polite. It wasn't about testing the waters. It was claiming something we both already knew belonged to us. My heart thundered against my ribs. It was dizzying, the way we fit. The way his mouth moved with mine, like he already knew how I liked to be kissed. Like he'd imagined this as many times as I had. It was fire and gravity. A match held too long to paper—far too late to stop it from catching.

And underneath it all, threaded through the fire, was something terrifyingly fragile. Hope.

Hope that this meant something. That we weren't just playing at fantasy behind masks and midnight.

The kiss said everything we hadn't. Every longing. Every what if. Every yes we hadn't gotten to say.

And I didn't want it to end.

By the time he pulled back—slowly, like it physically pained him—my lungs were dragging in air like I'd forgotten how to breathe.

He touched my cheek, fingers soft but sure. "Okay." His voice rumbled like gravel. "Into the car with you. Wanna make sure you're safe."

Reluctantly, I opened the door and slid into the driver's seat. I didn't want to leave. Didn't want to break whatever this was between us.

He took my hand one last time and lifted it to his lips, pressing a kiss to my knuckles. He lingered there, slow and reverent, as if he was committing the feel of my skin to memory. I wanted to close my eyes to do the same, but I didn't dare.

"Goodnight."

The word clung to my skin like a promise I wanted to chase.

"Goodnight."

He stepped back, shutting the door himself. Then he made the locking gesture, and waited— watchful, steady—as I clicked the locks and started the engine.

With one last double tap of the hood in farewell, he was gone.

He vanished surprisingly fast for a guy built like a Mack truck.

Goodbye, Cinderfella.

My lips quirked with the thought even as his

sudden absence snapped the spell, glitter turning to glass underfoot. Arms hugged across my middle, I turned on the heat, and then sat for a long minute. I wasn't cold. Not really. But I wanted to cling to the lingering sensation of Ramsey's arms around me, to the tingle on my knuckles where he'd kissed them and made me swoon. To the feeling of giddy possibility still bubbling inside me like champagne.

Eventually, I eased the car into gear, driving on autopilot while my thoughts stayed tangled in a tuxedo and a mask and the way he'd looked at me like I was something rare. Campus blurred past, quiet and soft around the edges, like the night itself was holding its breath with me. I didn't turn on the radio. I didn't need anything else filling the silence on the drive to Blair's.

I was still floating by the time I knocked. She opened her apartment door, and I stepped inside with a breath that wasn't quite a sigh, my hand curled around my clutch. I could still feel the imprint of his fingers tangled with mine. Still taste the kiss that had made everything inside me feel dizzy and new.

My bestie took one look at me and grinned like the cat who'd discovered the cream. "Oh, my God. You look like you just got kissed and liked it."

I bit back the smile that threatened to give me

away and turned toward the wall of silver-screen goddess movie posters that dominated her living room as if they were suddenly fascinating. "Maybe."

She snorted and danced in front of me on bare feet. "Girl. Maybe?" She stretched the word with delighted, scandalized disbelief. "No. No, no. That smile is not a maybe. That's a ten-out-of-ten, would-kiss-again, let's-do-something-stupid smile."

I didn't answer right away. Mostly because I was still trying to figure out how to explain something I hadn't fully let myself believe yet. Something that still felt delicate and private, like a secret I hadn't decided whether I was allowed to keep or share.

"Thanks for loaning me your car. It was good to be able to leave when I wanted. Can you give me a lift home? I'm pretty beat."

"Of course, sugar plum. But don't think you're getting out of the interrogation."

We reversed, heading back out of the apartment to her RAV-4 and piling in. Blair didn't even wait until the red light at the end of her street.

"So." She dragged the syllable out like a threat. "Start talking. I want every detail. Did he have a name? Did he have a face? Was he hot or only mas-querade-magic hot?"

I laughed, soft and still a little dazed, letting my

head tip back against the seat. The interior of the car was warm and a little stuffy, and I was still floating in that weird space between memory and fantasy where everything felt too beautiful to touch.

"There was a guy," I admitted. "Stranger in a mask." He hadn't been a stranger at all. Not really. But that detail felt too precious to reveal.

Blair let out a delighted gasp. "Finally."

"We danced." My voice drifted with the rhythm of the road. "We kissed."

Blair made a sound that could only be described as a full-body squee and thumped the steering wheel. "How was it?"

I exhaled a long, contented sigh. "He kissed me like a secret."

Blair squealed again. "You're getting positively lyrical. You should write that down."

"Maybe I will." Along with the rest of this personal fairy tale.

"And then what?"

A little of the glow faded. "And then he left."

Her head whipped in my direction. "Wait, what? Left?"

"Had somewhere to be." Of course, he hadn't said where, but I knew it must've been important. Because I knew him.

"That's it?" she demanded. "You're gonna drop that like a mic and move on?"

I smiled, still staring out the passenger window, watching our sleepy college campus blur past. "It was late."

"And mysterious."

"And magical." I hadn't meant to say that out loud, but it was true.

Blair's eyes cut toward me, sharp even as she turned. "Okay, so are you seeing him again?"

My heart tripped over itself at the question. "I don't know." It wasn't as if we'd made plans. Or as if either of us had been willing to break the alleged anonymity of the masks. Because reality was complicated.

She frowned. "Well, did you get his name at least?"

I hesitated, lips twitching. "No."

Blair's groan was dramatic enough to rival any theater kid. "Alia. *What* were you thinking?"

I didn't answer. Only smiled to myself and let my fingers drift to the edge of the clutch in my lap. I already knew. Surely he did, too.

Blair gave me a sideways look, exasperated but not unkind. "So what now? You wait and hope the Universe hands him back to you?"

I shrugged, still smiling, eyes tracking the soft wash of streetlights across the windshield. "Something like that."

Blair pulled up to the curb and shifted into

park with a flourish, throwing the car into neutral like she was dropping me off after a covert mission. She leaned across the console and shot me a grin. "Text me if he shows up on your doorstep. Or breaks into your dreams. Either way, I want details."

I rolled my eyes, but smiled as I unbuckled and reached for the door. "Night, Blair."

"Good night, mysterious masked maiden."

I shut the door behind me and waved once before the RAV-4 pulled away, her taillights fading down the street. The quiet that followed wrapped around me like a blanket, the sudden stillness both calming and welcome after the noise of the masquerade.

The front steps creaked under my heels as I climbed them, letting myself into the apartment. The lights were off. Bodie wasn't home yet, and I was absurdly glad for the emptiness. If he'd been here, he'd have taken one look at me and known. Not only that something had happened, but what. He always knew. And I wasn't ready to say it out loud. Not yet. Saying it made it real, and I was still floating in that in-between space where everything was too precious to touch.

The door shut behind me with a soft click, and I paused in the entryway, exhaling slowly. The mask was still on; the ties pulling slightly at the back of my head where I'd knotted them hours ago. I reached up, hesitated, then let my hand fall.

Not yet.

I moved on autopilot through the apartment, kicking off my heels with a sigh of relief. I padded toward my bedroom, clutch still in hand, mask still on, heart still beating like I'd danced all the way home.

Inside my room, I let the door close behind me and flicked on the overhead light. The sudden illumination felt stark. I dialed it down to the bedside lamp instead, letting the rest of the room stay swathed in shadow.

The mask came off first. I untied the ribbon and slid it away from my face, letting the cool satin trail across my fingers. I stared at it for a long moment before setting it gently on the dresser, like it might still be holding some residual charge from the night. Like it was fragile and important and maybe a little bit holy.

Then the dress—unzip, slide down, fold over the back of my desk chair. Each motion deliberate. As if I was trying not to disturb whatever spell might still be clinging to my skin.

I padded into the bathroom and flipped on the light. It buzzed softly, fluorescent and unforgiving. Still, I leaned in toward the mirror. Earrings and necklace off. Lipstick wiped away with a tissue that caught the ghost of his kiss. Then I scrubbed away the rest of my war paint with oil-based cleanser and rinsed away the last of the armor.

The girl in the mirror didn't look that different. Same long-lashed eyes, same sharp cheekbones, same stubborn mouth. But she felt different. Like maybe something had shifted behind her eyes. Like maybe she wasn't only pretending to be fearless anymore.

I studied myself a little longer, then turned off the light.

Still barefoot, still humming with aftershocks, I crossed back into my room, swapping the fancy underwear for my most comfortable pajamas before I crawled into bed and reached for my phone. I stared at the lock screen for a long moment, then opened the messaging app.

No new texts.

Of course not.

I know it was you. I hovered over the keyboard for a second, even typed out a single letter before deleting it.

What if I was wrong? I mean, I knew I wasn't. I knew down to my marrow it had been Ramsey. But on the infinitesimal chance it hadn't been...

He'd had the chance to reveal himself, and he hadn't taken it. Maybe he had reasons for that. I suspected I shared DNA with at least some of them.

If this was real—if it had meant something—he'd find me. The next move was his.

I set the phone aside, burrowed under the covers, and let myself smile, still feeling the whisper of his kiss. It hadn't been a dream. And I wasn't ready to let go of that yet.

Chapter 11

Ramsey

The truck's engine ticked as it cooled, the only sound in the otherwise quiet parking lot. I sat there for a beat, hand still on the keys, the scent of turf and sweat clinging to my skin like a second uniform. The regional combine had wrapped earlier that afternoon—a blur of timed sprints, verticals, shuttle drills, and interviews with scouts in branded polos who looked at me like a stat sheet in cleats. Three days of pressure cocked down into forty-yard dashes and broad jumps and questions about whether I had the mindset to go pro.

I'd nailed it. At least, that's what Langston said. I'd landed on the shortlist. And if all went well, I'd be invited to the national combine next. The one that could change everything.

My duffel bag was still slumped in the back seat, untouched since I left the field house. I hadn't been home yet. Hadn't showered. Hadn't eaten anything that didn't come vacuum-sealed. My whole body was heavy with exhaustion, but somehow still wired. Like my muscles hadn't caught up to my brain, or maybe the other way around.

But it wasn't the combine running laps through my brain. Not the scouts or the stats or what came next. It was Alia.

That kiss—God, that kiss—had been living rent free in my head since the second I walked away. Not the first one, soft and hesitant and sweet like a secret we weren't supposed to share. The second one. The one in the parking lot under the glare of the streetlights, when she'd looked at me like I was something worth holding onto, and said "God yes" before I could even finish the question.

That kiss hadn't felt like a maybe. It hadn't felt like pretending.

It felt like everything I'd ever wanted and never let myself name. Her mouth on mine, warm and sure and so damned open. Like she wanted it just as badly. As if maybe she'd been waiting, too. That kiss had hit me straight in the chest and rewired something I didn't know could change.

And I hadn't been the same since.

I kept replaying it, over and over. The slide of her hands into my jacket. The way she'd leaned into me without hesitation. The way it felt like falling—but somehow safe. I kept telling myself it hadn't meant more than the moment. That we were playing roles. That she didn't know it was me.

But that lie was getting harder to hold on to every time I closed my eyes and still felt her against me.

And now, after the biggest shot of my career, after three days of being hyped and tested and pushed to the edge of what my body could give, the only thing I wanted was to see her again. To know if it had meant something to her, too.

To know if maybe it hadn't only changed me.

I told myself I'd come here for Bodie. It was tradition. We always checked in after big games, after big milestones. This was the biggest one yet. He'd want to know how it went. He'd want the full play-by-play.

But it was really about her.

I hadn't been able to stop wondering if she hated me for walking away. If she thought I was just another guy too chickenshit to follow through. Or worse, if she thought I hadn't felt anything at all. Although surely after that kiss—

I had to talk to Bodie. Not just because he was my best friend. Because he was her brother. Her twin. Because if I was going to cross this line—really cross it—I needed to do it right.

Even if I already knew what he was going to say.

That I was too close. Too important. That if I screwed this up—and let's be honest, relationships ended more often than they didn't—it wouldn't just break her heart. It'd blow up everything. Bodie had trusted me with his family, with his sister, because he believed I'd never cross that line. And I hadn't. Not once. Not until now.

But I'd done it with eyes wide open. Because pretending I didn't feel what I felt wasn't working anymore. Because that kiss, that night, had meant something. And if there was even a chance that she wanted this too, I had to be man enough to face what came next.

With a long breath, I opened the door and stepped out into the cool night, the gravel crunching beneath my boots. The porch light over their duplex glowed faintly, the same as it always had, and I started toward it with something like dread and hope tangled together in my chest.

Bodie answered the door looking like he'd barely survived a minor war—sweatpants, hoodie from our freshman season, and a half-empty sports drink in hand. His hair stuck up like he'd been horizontal all afternoon and just remembered the existence of gravity.

He grinned when he saw me. "Dude. You made it back alive."

I let him pull me into a one-armed hug, the familiar slap of his palm against my back grounding me for a second. I didn't realize how much I needed that until it happened.

"Barely." I stepped inside.

The living room looked the same. Low lamplight, a blanket tossed over the couch, the faint scent of lavender and lemon from whatever candle Alia always had burning. My eyes scanned the room automatically, zeroing in on the details that mattered. No shoes by the door. No bag on the armchair. No soft rustle of movement from down the hall.

No Alia.

Relief and disappointment tangled in my chest, sharp and conflicting. I told myself it was better this way. That if she'd been here with all that glossy brown hair down, soft sweater, bare feet padding into the room like some kind of casual dream, I might've lost my nerve. Or worse, I might've kissed her again. And then what?

Bodie was already halfway to the kitchen. "Alia's out with Blair—some late-night indie movie. You know the kind. Lots of long stares and a metaphor you don't get till the credits roll. If you get it at all. Give me a good action flick any day."

I exhaled slowly through my nose. "Cool. That's... yeah."

Better this way. We'd have privacy for what was sure to be an awkward conversation.

"So?" He tossed me a Gatorade and leaned his hip against the counter. "How was it?"

I rolled the bottle between my hands, condensation slick against my skin. "Good." My voice came out quieter than I meant it to. "Better than good, actually. My verticals were clean. Forty shaved down to a 4.48. Talked to reps from three teams. Langston thinks I'll get a national invite this spring."

Bodie blinked. "Holy shit."

I looked up. He was staring at me like he hadn't heard me right, or maybe like he had and didn't quite know what to do with it.

"You serious?"

I gave him a small nod. "Yeah. They liked what they saw."

"Dude," he breathed. "That's—Ramsey, that's huge."

I shrugged, trying for nonchalance. "It's not the draft. But it's a shot. One of the few that actually count."

He straightened, eyes sharper now, no trace of

the usual sarcasm. "That's more than a shot. That's your foot in the goddamn door."

I gave a quiet laugh, mostly to cover the noise in my own chest. "Yeah. I guess."

He frowned. "You don't sound like a guy who just crushed one of the biggest weekends of his life."

I opened my mouth. Closed it again.

Because the truth was, even with the biggest break of my career sitting in my back pocket, the only thing I wanted to talk about wasn't the combine. It was his sister.

"Just tired." It was a lame response, even if it was partly true.

The pause that followed sat too heavy between us. I used it to glance at my phone like I was checking something important. I wasn't. I just needed a second to get my footing before I asked the question that had been riding me since I the moment I got off the field.

"So..." I tried for casual, leaning back against the counter and taking a sip of the Gatorade I didn't want. "How's Alia doing?"

Bodie wasn't looking at me. He was too busy grabbing a bowl from the cabinet and pouring himself a midnight mountain of Cinnamon Toast Crunch like we were still nineteen and cramming for finals. "Better." He opened the fridge again with his hip. "Party helped. I think the whole warrior queen vibe reminded her she's the badass in this equation."

I huffed a breath through my nose, the corner of my mouth tipping up. "Glad she's getting back to herself."

"She deserves better than what she's had. No more football players, man." He said it offhand, not even looking at me as he dumped milk on his cereal. But the words landed like they'd been aimed at center mass.

I went still. My grip on the bottle tightened, and for half a second I felt my pulse spike with panic. Did he know? Was this some kind of warning? A subtle way of telling me he'd figured it out?

But Bodie just shrugged and kept talking, still focused on the cereal in front of him like he hadn't just ripped the floor out from under me.

"Half the team are dogs," he muttered. "And the good ones—guys like you—you're gonna be headed for the pros. Always gone. Never around. She needs someone who's there, you know?"

I swallowed, but it did nothing to ease the pressure building in my throat. His words hit harder than he could've known.

Because he wasn't wrong.

Alia deserved someone who was steady. Who could show up and keep showing up. Who wouldn't miss birthdays or calls or bad days. Who wouldn't hide behind game schedules and travel days and excuses.

She needed someone who could offer a full heart, not just borrowed time. And God help me, I wanted to be that guy.

But I wasn't. Not now. Maybe not ever. Because if the combine meant what I thought it did—if the calls started coming in—my whole life was about to change. Again.

And Alia? She'd be left waiting. Wanting. And I'd be the reason she never got what she deserved. Because I could give her almost everything—but not all of it. Not the part that mattered most. Not my undivided time and attention.

I nodded like it didn't hurt. Like my chest wasn't folding in on itself with every word Bodie said. I leaned back against the counter and took another drink, letting the Gatorade wash down the lump in my throat. Because what could I say? He wasn't wrong. He was just... saying it without knowing the target he'd hit.

I'd come here stupidly hoping that I could find some clarity. That I could talk to Bodie and maybe figure out a way to tell him. To admit that I had feelings for his sister. That she was so much more to me than a friend. That I wanted that more. That I thought she felt the same.

But now? Now I knew I couldn't. Because if I

really gave a damn about Alia—and I did, more than I could say—then I didn't get to be selfish. I didn't get to hold on to a fantasy that was always going to fall apart the minute the season ended and the draft began.

She'd kissed me like I mattered. Like I was more than the guy who'd always been just out of reach. And I'd kissed her like I wanted everything. Because I did. I wanted her laughter and her fire and her quiet moments when no one was looking. I wanted a future I hadn't even dared imagine before that night.

But a kiss—no matter how perfect—couldn't outrun reality. I was leaving. Maybe not tomorrow, but soon enough. And she deserved someone who stayed.

So I kept my mouth shut. Let Bodie keep talking about her like I wasn't already breaking apart. Because if I told him now, it would be asking for something I wasn't allowed to have. It would be planting hope in soil that couldn't grow anything lasting.

I wouldn't do that to her. I couldn't. She deserved the whole damn world. And all I could give her was goodbye. I had to pretend that I hadn't known. That she really had been a stranger. That the fantasy hadn't been everything I could possibly want.

I left not long after. Mumbled something about needing sleep, and that I'd catch up later. Bodie didn't question it. He just clapped me on the shoulder, then held out a fist for the bump we always traded. I gave it to him, solid and sure, even though my whole chest felt like it was splintering.

Once I was inside my truck, I didn't start the engine right away. I just sat there, staring straight ahead into the dark, the quiet hum of the night settling around me. My duffel sat forgotten in the backseat. My hands rested on my thighs, empty and twitching like they didn't know what to do now that they weren't holding her.

I looked up—just once—into the rearview mirror. My face stared back, all shadow and scruff. I was supposed to feel like a rising star. Like a guy whose whole future had just shifted into high gear. But all I felt like was a man who'd let something perfect slip through his fingers. Something he might never get back.

And maybe I was doing the right thing. Maybe this was what love looked like when you did it unselfishly. Quiet. Sacrificial.

But it didn't feel noble. It felt like grief.

Still, I turned the key. Let the engine rumble to life. Told myself the lies I'd need to survive it. That one night could be enough. That the memory would be enough. That she'd be okay. And I would be too. Eventually.

But God, it didn't feel that way as I pulled out of the lot and disappeared into the dark.

* * *

Hold the tomatoes!

I know. I know. This isn't how you wanted this story to end. But I warned you in the beginning! That's why it's a PREQUEL. Because their story isn't over!

They walked away without ever saying what mattered most. But some sparks don't burn out—no matter how many years, secrets, or miles lie between them.

Catch your breath now. Because in *Hero Ever After*, Alia and Ramsey are about to collide all over again. Don't miss Book 1 in the brand new Gibson Hollow series, releasing August 22nd!

I never meant to be anyone's heroine.

Not when I became the acting mayor of my hometown after the flood. Not when I kept my law practice afloat out of a booth in my grandmother's diner. And definitely not when my secret romantasy novels went viral.

Nobody in Gibson Hollow knows I'm the author behind the pen name. And nobody was supposed to kiss me at that book convention—**least of all my brother's best friend, cosplaying the hero he doesn't know I modeled after him.**

Now Ramsey Shaw is back in town. Volunteering. Smiling at me like I'm not on the verge of shattering. Like he remembers the kiss. Like he sees the truth.

I've spent my whole life being strong. Quiet. In control. But for the first time, I don't want to be any of those things.

I just want to be his.

In a town held together by hope and heart, it's the people who show up that make it shine.

Grab your copy of *Hero Ever After today!*

In the meantime, are you looking for another series to sink your teeth into? Don't miss the *Men of the Misfit Inn*, beginning with *Let It Be Me*.

Other Books By Kait Nolan

A complete and up-to-date list of all my books can be found at https:// kaitnolan.com.

GIBSON HOLLOW
SMALL TOWN SOUTHERN ROMANCE

- Hero After Midnight (prequel)
- Hero Ever After (Alia and Ramsey)
  Coming August 22th

**KILTED HEARTS
SMALL TOWN CONTEMPORARY SCOTTISH
ROMANCE**

- *Jilting The Kilt* (prequel)
- *Cowboy in a Kilt* (Raleigh and Kyla)
- *Grump in a Kilt* (Malcolm and Charlotte)
- *Playboy in a Kilt* (Connor and Sophie)
- *Protector in a Kilt* (Ewan and Isobel)
- *Single Dad in a Kilt* (Hamish and Afton)
- *Kilty Pleasures* (Jason and Skye)

SPECIAL OPS SCOTS
SMALL TOWN MILITARY SCOTTISH ROMANCE

- *One Fine Night* (prequel)
- *Before Highland Sunset* (Alex and Ciara)
- *Beyond Highland Sunrise* (Callum and Parker)
- *Beneath Highland Stars* (Finley and Saoirse)

BAD BOY BAKERS
SMALL TOWN MILITARY ROMANCE

- *Rescued By a Bad Boy* (Brax and Mia prequel)
- *Mixed Up With a Marine* (Brax and Mia)

- *Wrapped Up with a Ranger* (Holt and Cayla)
- *Stirred Up by a SEAL* (Jonah and Rachel)
- *Hung Up on the Hacker* (Cash and Hadley)
- *Caught Up with the Captain* (Grey and Rebecca)

RESCUE MY HEART SERIES
SMALL TOWN MILITARY ROMANCE

- *Someone Like You* (Ivy and Harrison)
- *What I Like About You* (Laurel and Sebastian)
- *Bad Case of Loving You* (Paisley and Ty prequel) Included in *Made For Loving You* (Paisley and Ty)

THE MISFIT INN SERIES
SMALL TOWN FAMILY ROMANCE

- *When You Got A Good Thing* (Kennedy and Xander)
- *Til There Was You* (Misty and Denver)
- *Those Sweet Words* (Pru and Flynn)
- *Stay A Little Longer* (Athena and Logan)

* *Bring It On Home* (Maggie and Porter)
* *Come Away with Me* (Moses and Zuri)

MEN OF THE MISFIT INN
SMALL TOWN SOUTHERN ROMANCE

* *Let It Be Me* (Emerson and Caleb)
* *Our Kind of Love* (Abbey and Kyle)
* *Don't You Wanna Stay* (Deanna and Wyatt)
* *Until We Meet Again* (Samantha and Griffin prequel)
* *Come A Little Closer* (Samantha and Griffin)
* *Just Wanted You To Know* (Livia and Declan)
* *A Love Like You* (Juliette and Mick)

WISHFUL ROMANCE SERIES
SMALL TOWN SOUTHERN ROMANCE

* *To Get Me To You* (Cam and Norah)
* *Know Me Well* (Liam and Riley)
* *Be Careful, It's My Heart* (Brody and Tyler)
* *The Matchmaker Maneuver* (Myles and Piper prequel)

- *Just For This Moment* (Myles and Piper)
- *Wish I Might* (Reed and Cecily)
- *Turn My World Around* (Tucker and Corinne)
- *Dance Me A Dream* (Jace and Tara)
- *See You Again* (Trey and Sandy)
- *The Christmas Fountain* (Chad and Mary Alice)
- *You Were Meant For Me* (Mitch and Tess)
- *A Lot Like Christmas* (Ryan and Hannah)
- *Dancing Away With My Heart* (Zach and Lexi)

WISHFUL MOMENTS SERIES
BITE-SIZED WISHFUL ROMANCE

- *Once Upon A Coffee* (Avery and Dillon)
- *Once Upon A Rescue* (Brooke and Hayden)
- *Who I Am with You* (Dinah and Robert)

WISHING FOR A HERO SERIES (A WISHFUL SPINOFF SERIES)

SMALL TOWN ROMANTIC SUSPENSE

- *Make You Feel My Love* (Judd and Autumn)
- *Watch Over Me* (Nash and Rowan)
- *Can't Take My Eyes Off You* (Ethan and Miranda)
- *Burn For You* (Sean and Delaney)

MEET CUTE ROMANCE
SMALL TOWN SHORT ROMANCE

- *Once Upon A Snow Day*
- *Once Upon A New Year's Eve*
- *Once Upon An Heirloom*

SUMMER FLING TRILOGY
CONTEMPORARY ROMANCE

- *Second Chance Summer*
- *Summer Camp Secret*
- *The Summer Camp Swap*

About Kait

Kait is a Mississippi native, who often swears like a sailor, calls everyone sugar, honey, or darlin', and can wield a bless your heart like a saber or a Snuggie, depending on requirements.

You can find more information on this *USA Today* best selling and RITA ® Award-winning author and her books on her website http://kaitnolan.com.

About Kait

Do you need more small town sass and spark? Sign up for <u>her newsletter</u> to hear about new releases, book deals, and exclusive content!